I Shall Know Who I Am

I Shall Know Who I Am

Norman Finn

Mill City Press

Mill City Press, Inc.
2301 Lucien Way #415
Maitland, FL 32751
407.339.4217
www.millcitypress.net

Printed in the United States of America

ISBN-13: 9781545630396

DEDICATION

For my wife, Judith, and our children, Ted and Rachel

"Duty is doing the right thing, at the right time, for the right
reason without regards to the cost of one's self"
Angelo Duks

ACKNOWLEDGMENTS

Working on the book was a pure delight for it took me places I would have never discovered or re-visited.

I had unlimited support from friends and family during its creation.

My wife, Judith, who is in the midst of the middles stages of Alzheimer's, was always there to help in every way. There were bumps in the road along the way; the death of my older brother, Ben, and unforeseen family medical issues. At times, it was a question mark whether it would get finished.

Without the effort of Marge Keohane it would not have come to life. She transposed my hieroglyphics into a readable manuscript.

Listed below are the major sources that I would like to identify. Without them and internet research, "I Shall Know Who I Am" would not have come to life.

Inside Israel's Mossad	Matt Webster
Nasser and the Missile Age in the Middle East	Owen Sirrs
NY Time: Old Nazi's Never Die	Nicholas Kulish
Gideon Spies: The Secret History of the Mossad	Thomas Gudrum

The Complete Pyramids	Mark Lehner
Nasser: A Political Biography	Stephen Roberts
Jerusalem: One City, Three Faiths	Karen Armstrong
Egyptian Cotton	Crane and Canopy
Military Explosives	Google Books
Introduction to Explosives	Jared Ledgard
This is Jerusalem	Menashe Har'el
The Egyptian Museum	Waffa El-Saddik
Alexandria	Collins Dictionary
El Alamein	C.E. Lucas Phillips
The Middle East from the End of the Empire to the End of the Cold War	P.J. Vatikiotis
The Decline of Arab Unity: Rise and Fall of the UAR	Elie Podeh
The Spies: Israel's Counter-Espionage War	Yossi Melman, Eitan Haber
And the Internet	

CHAPTER ONE

HIS DAD, KARL JANSSEN, GREW UP JUST OUTSIDE DES
Moines, Iowa, in a windswept farming town called Hartford. There
was a local grocery store and gas station, not much more. Their
back yard was a vast glimmering cornfield that went on as far as the
eye could see. It seemed at times to be an endless golden-green sea
waving in the wind.

It was not an easy place to live, with deep, penetrating cold that
froze the locks on the garage, to searing heat that made it impossible
to touch the backhoe. Besides, it was challenging times for everyone.
The world of the 1920s was moving toward the Great Depression
and uncharted waters.

He had God-fearing parents wedded to the land who had a deep
sense of faith and love of country. Karl was a master mechanic who
would not only fix your automobile but also your washing machine.
He tinkered with anything that had a motor, and was happiest with
industrial grease under his fingernails.

He fell in love and married Anna—a fine, handsome woman
almost the height of her husband. She was a pillar of strength in their
home and community, always finding a way to weather the storms of
adversity. She essentially was the "glue" that held the family together.
Anna taught school before they were married and was constantly
pushing their son to achieve a higher level of learning.

David was their only child, a product of German-Dutch heritage and midwestern values. A "big kid" for his age, he seemed to grow up quickly, always playing sports with boys two to four years older than him. He was more than six feet tall, with an athletic build, fair skin, blue eyes, blondish locks, and a persona that read "WASP" through and through.

David grew up in an atmosphere of love and commitment to excellence. He was everyone's high school hero, being captain of the basketball team and president of his class. He was an integral part of the community as his parents and family had been for generations. Together with his academic record and his basketball ability, David secured a full scholarship to the state university. He was considered the all-American boy!

He was more than a good student and showed exceptional aptitude in math and the sciences. All this translated into receiving a fellowship to graduate school, where he majored in engineering. David interviewed and applied to a number of graduate programs. He was totally surprised when he was accepted into the MIT program. Boston/Cambridge opened a whole new world and gave him a multifaceted education. The university brought out the best in him, enabling him to unlock his hidden talents and grow in every area.

Summers were spent with Kruger International, an engineering firm in Chicago. The "country" mentality that was prevalent in Iowa gave way to a new sophistication and self-confidence. He was in his element and devoured every opportunity to develop.

Most women found him hard to resist. His clean-cut, midwestern manner was a major asset. David had the kind of personality that always won you over. He was in a city full of young people, all of them willing to try new opportunities and new ventures. After graduate school, he became a full-time employee of Kruger and started to climb the organizational ladder.

More than four thousand miles away, Hannah Houran came from an entirely different world. Her parents and family had lived in Egypt for generations. There was some question in their history as to whether they came from Iraq or Yemen. They had relatives throughout the Middle East, and it was possible to trace the family tree back to the Holy Land. All were involved in the import/export business and traded through their family ties from Baghdad, Damascus, and Beirut.

Her father, Abraham, the patriarch of the family, was an accomplished scholar of antiquities. He spoke Hebrew, English, and two dialects of Arabic and was a man of noble character and integrity, which showed in every aspect of his life. Being a Jew in Egypt was not easy and demanded awareness in every component of life:—social, economic, and political.

Hannah's mother, Chaia, had the business mind for the family. She ran the company, giving her husband the opportunity to study the humanities and the Torah. As most Sephardic Jews, they were close. History had scattered them throughout the ancient world, which demanded family unity.

Hannah cut a striking pose, with magnificent poise and balance, blue eyes that seemed to have an inner light, and long black hair that framed her dark skin. She was tall and statuesque, and heads turned when she walked by. She was the oldest and had a brother and sister three years apart.

Her father gave her his genes, for she had his skills in the humanities, languages, and sensitivity. They spoke two dialects of Arabic at home, depending on whether they were speaking about Egypt or their Iraqi relatives or business.

Hannah was enrolled at the British International School in Cairo, where she showed great promise in all her studies and especially in the arts. She was extremely talented in painting and drawing, but her real passion was art history. Hannah had a difficult time winning over her parents in allowing her to go off to study in London. She was a beautiful, unmarried Jewish woman brought up in a strict household that not only had a Jewish mentality but also Arab mores and customs. It was quite unusual that she could do this. Schooling in London gave her a totally unique perspective on how she wanted to live her life. Her feelings for the arts gave her a special level of sensitivity.

David found the position and company to his liking and put his entire energy into building his reputation and résumé. He was recognized as an "up-and-coming" product. His star was rising, and he attained an executive position rather quickly. His first projects were in the States, and slowly his level of expertise showed immense progress. The results were a senior management position and assignments overseas. He was building a reputation and was rewarded with numerous projects around the globe. His moving around the world brought him on-the-job experience. He became one of the Kruger Engineering key executives.

Hannah did not want to return to Egypt when her education ended. She had become a "liberated lady," which was exactly the lifestyle she could not assume on her return to Cairo. The rules were quite different on what she could or could not do. She had spent more than three years in London and was a different person than the one who left. She wanted to live a Westernized type of life." The edict came down from her parents to return home. The decision was final.

It was the beginning of a conflict between Hannah and her parents. She loved them dearly, but she wanted to defend and participate in a new lifestyle so foreign to them. How could she explain the new, energizing world she had been part of? She would not defy them and came home.

Hannah was not only exquisite but extremely bright and entrepreneurial. Her schooling and talent opened doors that were normally closed to the average Egyptian woman. Her art training brought a prestigious position with the Art Institute in Cairo.

David's assignments had taken him to the European theater. It was a hydroelectric plant in Norway or infrastructures in the Netherlands. Management had just won a major contract for a water-treatment facility in Cairo. David was going to lead the team as the key executive for Kruger. It would be a long, complicated project that meant a year or two in Egypt.

As an eligible Chicago bachelor, he had dated and spent time with many women. At the point of a serious commitment, David was off to the next project thousands of miles away. Nothing came of any of these romances, for he was always on the move. The ladies showed great interest but wanted commitment. David was off to the next project thousands of miles away. His apartment in Chicago was hardly used. The takeaway on David by his circle of friends was that he was a "free spirit" and not ready for a serious relationship. David was one of the most eligible, but his reputation was very elusive, distant, and only available for the short run.

Bags packed once again, David flew TWA to Cairo. He had read about the city and country and was looking forward to this new experience. The sights, sounds, and aromas of Cairo were so foreign to him. He was excited, amazed, and captured by the city and his work. The company had experience setting up their employees overseas. Everything was arranged, and his accommodations were more than adequate. He started the project immediately and became totally absorbed in his work. At the same time, he wanted to understand the culture, the people, and the mentality of Egypt. His main problem was coping with the humidity and heat, changing his shirt two to three times a day. The office was away from the actual worksite, adjacent to the Said Palace, which housed the Modern Egyptian Art Museum.

Upon Hannah's return, she attained an executive position at the Modern Egyptian Art Museum. She had found her haven, and it was the perfect fit. The training in London, along with her innate talent in art history, made the position very fulfilling. Her forced return to Egypt was more than softened by being enthused in her work.

She showed a high level of artistic ingenuity putting the collections together. Modern art in Egypt could not compete with antiquities. Her work brought the collections to life, making it more attractive to those who came to see the displays. Hannah made the pieces stand out with her firsthand knowledge. Egyptian artists such as Muktar and Said were given additional recognition because of Hannah's firsthand knowledge, attention, and creativity.

David worked with the office windows wide open, hoping to catch some of the occasional breezes that came off the terrace. His office was on the second floor overlooking a piazza that was adjacent to the museum. It was the noon hour, and he wandered out on the terrace to see the city in motion. The piazza was cloistered from the traffic and constant bustle of Cairo. The shadows of the structures surrounding the piazza gave it some protection from the noonday sun, and the fountain in the center gave a misty, cooling spray. It had a seating area where many of the staff from the museum and his office building mingled, either taking a break with a coffee or eating their lunch.

Leaning on the wrought-iron banister, he saw Hannah. She was bathed in the noonday sun. Her striking pose captivated David from the moment he laid eyes on her. He became a regular at the piazza and, over a period of weeks, started a conversation with Hannah.

"I don't mean to intrude, but I heard you speaking English. I am new to this city and country and curious about everything Egyptian."

"Oh, yes, my English seems to be sufficient and a necessity in my position at the museum."

"My name is David . . . David Janssen. As you can probably tell, I'm an American who doesn't know the first thing about this city and country."

"Oh, an American. I have a lot of interest in learning about your country. I have never been there but have lived and studied with your 'cousins' in the UK."

"Well, as you know, we had major differences with our 'cousins' in 1776, and now we love them from afar." They both laughed.

"My name is Hannah, and I welcome you to Cairo. So David, tell me about you."

He gave her a quick history of his upbringing and current situation.

"You seem to have your head on your shoulders, as we say in Arabic. I admire you for having the desire to go to a foreign land and culture and develop a life. It takes a special person to live that adventure."

"I don't know if it takes a special person, just a guy like me who doesn't know any better." They both laughed. "Maybe you can show me some of the city and we could have lunch or dinner."

"Let's see if that can be worked out."

So after that first meeting, it seemed that both parties could not wait to see each other at lunch or taking a coffee in the late afternoon. They were drawn to one another as if it was some sort of destiny.

David was totally in love for the first time. It was hard to explain, for it came from within and consumed him. He was lost for words. Here was a Jewess, a gorgeous Egyptian creature who just changed his entire world overnight. David didn't know how to proceed, and Hannah was equally smitten. Here was an American Protestant whose world was so different from hers that it could not be put into words. She was in love and absolutely in turmoil over what to do about the situation. How could she explain to her family what was happening?

"David, we seem to be drawn to one another and, from an inno-cent meeting, we are now seeing each other on a regular basis. There are feelings between us that bring on a whole set of problems. We are from two different worlds, not just four thousand miles apart but from an ideology five thousand years old."

"Hannah, I realize the differences, but both of us live in the present. We both know that if there is a real, true bond between us, no problem can change our goals. You and I are the same. We do not think like our parents, who are pillars of their society and upbringing. I am involved with today's world, and my way of life is based on what is before me, not in the past. I respect everything you are saying, but I cannot believe if two people love one another they cannot find a way to make life work in their favor."

"David, we are Jews. Our whole tradition is based on our faith and adhering not only to the laws of God but to our social responsibilities." She was torn between "tradition," faith, and her love for David.

He was brought up to be a good Christian but not in terms of being very devout. In his world, he had never seen a Jew until he attended college at MIT. David had some contact in Chicago through friends and business associates, and that was the extent of his interaction. Until Hannah, it didn't even cross his mind what you believed in. Religion was not a priority in his world. Having a life with Hannah was his goal, and nothing else mattered. He would even consider converting if it meant winning her.

Hannah's problems were deep-seated and centered around the family. They were Sephardic Jews, deeply religious but not ultra-Orthodox, committed to the faith and family. There wasn't any separation between family and religion in their minds, and compromise was not in their vocabulary.

The relationship could not be kept in the shadows. The Jewish community was not large, but one could not conduct a courtship in Cairo without being seen by friends and family. Her father was understanding to a point but was not willing to consider a deviation from his heritage, which meant Jewish, Egyptian, possibly Middle Eastern, and nothing else. Her mother, born and brought up in the tradition of an obedient wife and mother, stood with her husband. She was willing to bend if there was an immovable impasse, at least in secret.

David was in a difficult position and did not know how much pressure he should put on Hannah. He was prepared to do whatever was necessary to make her his wife. She was at the breaking point, torn between two worlds she so desperately wanted. He felt his work was suffering. The project was moving along nicely, but he was unhappy with his performance. He could not truly understand the Egyptian mentality and fought the system, which only responded to graft, political corruption, and bribery. It was a world David had never seen or believed existed. Nothing really happened unless you became part of the process. The combination of living and working in these conditions frustrated him. It was a learning experience that he was totally unaware of or prepared for. These factors were building in his thinking and were only accentuated by his desire to make a life with Hannah.

The impasse could not be broken. The family edict was maintaining the party line. Fall in love with your own! Be steadfast in keeping your heritage and your God in their correct places. Hannah was in the process of revolting against the family. They were lovers, and their desire for one another was insatiable, creating a strong bond between them even though religion was a factor. Their love for one another became the primary concern in their lives.

The family was not about to give up on Hannah and decided to use all their influence to have David leave the country. The joint venture company that worked with Kruger was enlisted to put added pressure on the relationship, and relatives were asked to speak to Hannah.

David, on the other hand, realized that he could lose her and decided on a different course of action. What was Judaism, and why did it have such a hold on its believers? Why was it so strong for her and her family? Was it that different from what he believed in? Why was the religion so encompassing that it covered every area of one's life?

David started to do his research. He was an engineer, and he went about the task of finding out the reasons why. When he went back to Chicago for corporate meetings, he contacted a Rabbi and they had several discussions, and David became a student of the religion. It became apparent to him there was now a reason to become a Jew more than just wanting Hannah. He felt the principles of Judaism exemplified the way he wanted to live his life.

He had been on the job in Cairo for two years, and his project had reached a point where his expertise was no longer needed. The major construction was done and it was now turning into a training mission to put local people into positions. The "winding down" phase was in full swing, and David realized that his tenure in Egypt would soon be coming to an end. Decision time was around the corner, and he felt his whole life was in jeopardy of disintegrating without Hannah. How do you come to grips with the situation? How do you figure out the way forward? How do you find the solution that will bring a life together with their love?

They decided to elope, to run away, to leave Egypt and return to Chicago. It was a heart-wrenching decision for Hannah, who loved and respected her family. They were so important in her life, but David was her love. She so much wanted their approval, their blessing. How could it be achieved by marrying out of the faith? How could she rationalize running away to another world, forsaking her family and their wishes? What was she doing, leaving her life, her culture, her country, her friends? It was a period of introspection covering every aspect of her life. Was she doing the right thing? It was the most difficult decision of her life. All the questions weighed upon her. David made all the arrangements for their departure.

Hannah was beside herself, being pulled in opposite directions at the same time.

She asked him if he would consider becoming a Jew. Hannah had no idea that David had contacted a Rabbi, studied, and was on the brink of telling her that he wanted to convert. She insisted their children would be raised as Jews. His promise made her decision to marry much easier and gave her the strength and motivation to seek a new life. So they slipped away from Egypt in the night and started their new life in a different world.

It was a new world for both! David came back to the Midwest a totally different person. He had spent more than two years in Egypt and became aware of a world with a culture, mentality, and attitude so foreign from his own. Some Middle Eastern mentality had rubbed off, and he could now bargain as an Egyptian, understand the language, and appreciate the cuisine, and he knew something about Jews.

They were married immediately by a judge at the home of dear friends. David's parents made the trek from Iowa. They had met Hannah only a week before, when David brought her to his hometown. Anna took Hannah aside and gave her the silver set that had been in her family for generations. Karl and Anna formed a bond almost immediately, which gave her a feeling of family.

"I hope the both of you will have a long and happy life. Karl and I have been fortunate to have found happiness together. We wish you the same."

Hannah called her father and broke the news. There was silence. Although he did not tear his collar and declare that their daughter was dead, he was devastated. Abraham announced she was no longer part of the family. There would be no contact with her, at least for the time being. It was a halfway measure. Hannah was heartbroken, hoping beyond hope there could be a reconciliation. David went back to work and began projects that were developed in the Chicago office. He scheduled no travel except day trips around the country. Acclimating Hannah to their new life, the city, the country, was his priority. Hannah had known adversity in her life, and despite her sorrow and conflict, she wanted this new beginning. It was an exciting time in a new world with David. Thoughts of Egypt and her family were still there, wanting to be resolved.

Chapter Two

We say time heals all wounds. They were together, extremely happy, and wanted to start a family. David reaffirmed his desire to convert, and Hannah realized that he could not handle the conversion process of Orthodox Judaism. They chose the Reform Movement and started conversion classes together. It was not only a learning experience for David, but Hannah became aware of her heritage and culture. She had a whole new perspective on her faith. Her father would not speak to her, but her mother would communicate. She did not know just how much was told to her dad.

David was gaining stature and was promoted to a senior position that involved overseeing projects around the world. His travel schedule was full, but he managed to keep the trips to within a reasonable length so he would not be away for any significant amount of time. Hannah became pregnant, and before they realized it, there was a beautiful daughter whom they named Rachel after David's aunt who had passed away. They had found their place in the community in a wonderful house on the north shore of Lake Michigan. David had lived up to his commitment and had gone through with the studies program for the conversion. Hannah was beside herself with joy. She could now inform the family that she was married to a Jew, that she had not discarded her Jewishness and heritage. She had been in constant contact with her mother over the years, but there still was a wall of silence with her father.

Hannah wanted to find a way to put her life back together with her family and decided to go to Egypt. David had a project in Europe and would take her there and then return to his work. It had been almost five years since she had seen her family. The emotional anticipation and excitement had been building for weeks.

The voyage was by sea over two weeks, reaching the Port of Alexandria, where the family met her. She had not seen them in five years and was returning with an eighteen-month old daughter and emotions that were hard to contain. Egypt was not the same, and the world was about to become a smoldering cauldron, overflowing, covering the face of the globe. The events in Europe were going to have a direct impact on her family and Egypt.

On her arrival, she was shocked at the change in her father and the overall conditions in Egypt. The Jewish population had decreased by 30 to 40 percent. They had moved to Israel and around the globe. The family business had come upon hard times, and the economic situation had changed drastically. Her father refused to leave his home and business. He was an Egyptian and would live out his days in Cairo. They could not convince the patriarch to come to the States or Israel. He still believed there was hope, and his life, friends, and business were there. Hannah was heartbroken, and even though her mother supported the move, her father prevailed.

Egypt was in total disarray at that time, and the problems had started years before. The British viewed Egypt as a strategic link to India. The Ottoman Turks, who were in control but whose power was waning, invited the British to play a more direct role. In 1875 Britain purchased the local Egyptian government's remaining shares of the Suez Canal. In 1882 an Egyptian revolt against the Turks and European domination was crushed by the British expeditionary force. This resulted in bringing Egypt within the sphere of the British Empire. The growing nationalism after World War I induced the UK to declare Egypt an independent state in 1922. They still dominated Egyptian politics and controlled all aspects of the fiscal, military, and government reforms. The 1930s were controlled directly and indirectly by the British Empire. Their emphasis was shown by moving their Mediterranean fleet from Malta to Alexandria. These were the conditions that were in place when Hannah arrived.

After being in Cairo more than three weeks, it was time to come home. She was visibly upset with the state of her family and Egypt. Hannah realized the family's lives were disintegrating and there was nothing she could do about it. She knew the world was getting out of control and pain and chaos would find their way to them and Egypt. She begged them to leave and go to Israel but really wanted them to come to the States. It was a sad parting, for it was impossible to predict whether they would see each other again. Money was left in the hope they would change their minds.

On her departure, Hannah reiterated her feelings. "My parents, we are concerned with your safety and well-being. Both of you are getting older, and Egypt is no longer the same as it was years ago. There is anti-Semitism in full view and the family business is having its issues. Let me take you to the United States or to Israel."

Life in her secure world of Chicago was good. David was a loving, loyal lover and friend, besides a wonderful father, and it was a good marriage. Rachel was almost five years old, and Hannah wanted another child. She became pregnant and they were overjoyed.

David had become a key asset to the firm and was in line for a top management position. His work, as before, was taking him worldwide. Hannah was not pleased with his new travel schedule, for she felt he could be in harm's way.

Michael was born right on time, a large baby with long legs and artistic fingers who was the pride of his dad. He was almost a Leap Year baby, for he was born on March 1, 1936. There were memorable events on that day. Adolf Hitler decided to annex the Rhineland. In that week, German divisions entered the Rhineland, voiding the Versailles Treaty that was formulated after Germany's defeat in World War I. The storm clouds were gathering.

David had to travel after Michael's circumcision ceremony. He had postponed the trip for eight weeks so that Hannah would get back on her feet. He felt he was not leaving her alone, for they had someone coming in to help daily. He booked the flight to Germany. David's company had a long-standing relationship with Siemens, located in Munich.

Chapter Three

How do you explain tragedy? There really isn't an explanation. It just arrives with a force that bleeds the soul and makes you lose all faith in God, at least for some time.

David arrived in the Munich office and started working on the project immediately. He had known Herr Schmidt, his equivalent at Siemens, for some time and could never understand why they called each other "Mr." It was that language and cultural thing that David could never fathom.

The staff was very cordial and extremely helpful in defining and solving the issues. They knew their business and went about it, leaving nothing to chance. Schmidt invited David to dinner along with some of their staff. They were very curious about America and asked David countless questions, ranging from politics to baseball, over numerous steins of the local brew. Somehow or another, one of the group wanted to know if America was having "ein Juden problem." David was not only astonished; he was angry and told the group just how he felt about the situation in Germany, ending by stating he was a Jew and proud of it. There was utter silence. In one moment, the room had gone from a normal atmosphere to an Arctic chill.

It was difficult to put a call through to the States in 1936. You had to place it with the international operator, and it could take two to eight hours for the call to come through. David wanted to speak to Hannah and Rachel and hear about the progress of his newborn son. He did not mention anything about the incident at dinner. Hannah wanted him home and kept asking when he would return.

"David, I have been following the situation in Germany and am very concerned about your safety. Besides you being a Jew, anyone not involved with the Nazis could be in harm's way."

"Hannah, I am very safe! Siemens is probably the safest place I can be in Germany. There is no reason to be worried."

Hannah spoke with a serious tone. "You are dismissing the severity of the situation. I have seen anti-Semitism in the flesh in Egypt and the rise of authorianism. Please take care."

"My love, don't worry about me. Everything is going along without a problem. I have another ten days here before everything on my end is finished. How are the kids? Can I speak to Rachel?" They talked further about the children.

Hitler's storm troopers, known as the "Brownshirts" helped his rise to power in the 1920s and '30s. They were meant to be the Nazi Army and represented anti-Semitic and anti-democratic thought. When Hitler rose to power in 1933, they became an official government organization. They set up concentration camps. They roamed Munich and terrorized anyone they wished, for they had the authority to do so.

It seemed there were Brownshirts everywhere he went. It was not a coincidence. They were there and wanted to know what he did and who, if anyone, he spoke with. There were always two of them, and they did not try to hide their presence. In fact, they made a point to silently inform him they were there.

He noticed that his room had been searched; clothing had not been put back in the same order. It was very apparent. Suddenly, no one spoke to him outside of the necessary conversation regarding the project. He was persona non grata, and it was intentional, cold, and calculated. They had to work with him, for they needed the support of Kruger, which he represented.

David now had little contact with anyone outside of his office hours at Siemens. He ate at the hotel and would either write or read to pass the time, seldom venturing out.

It was already May, and Munich was in bloom and full of life. The city was known for its annual Oktoberfest celebration and endless beer halls. There is the "Walkable," Old Town, Marienplatz, the Central Square, containing the landmarks of the city. Munich is the capital and largest city of Bavaria on the banks of the Isar River, north of the Bavarian Alps. It had a history of tension after World War I. In 1923 Hitler and his supporters were concentrated in Munich and attempted to overthrow and seize power of the Weimar Republic, established after the war. It failed, resulting in Hitler's arrest and setting back the Nazi Party, which was virtually unknown outside Munich. The city once again became a Nazi stronghold when the National Socialists took power in 1923. The party created its first concentration camp at Dachau, ten miles from the city. Munich was referred to as the capital of the Nazi movement.

David was nearing completion of his part of the project and wanted to see the city and surrounding area before departing. He walked the city in the evenings and weekends now that the weather was good. He stood outside the hotel one night as the Nazis, en masse, marched with lighted torches through the city chanting: "Heil Hitler! Death to the Jews! Deutchland uber alles!" their boots thundering over the cobblestones of the old town as their voices rang out in unison. David could not believe what he was seeing.

What was happening to this world? How could this possibly exist?

It was spring, but he turned up his coat collar, for he was chilled. The crowds watching cheered them on.

Bavaria was simply picturesque or for it had breathtaking views of the Alps, magnificent scenery, and quaint medieval towns. The border with Austria was very near, and more of the same existed. It also had a Nazi mentality and ideology on both sides of the border. All of Bavaria was pro-Hitler, anti-democratic, and anti-Semitic. The fuhrer was in total control.

He rented a car on the weekend and decided to see the Alps. David drove southeast toward Salzburg and the mountains. He needed a change of scenery, and the mountains pleased him. The kilometers mounted and he was soon at the Austrian border. The border crossing was not a problem.

Salzburg, which borders Germany, is a magical place. It is internationally renowned for its baroque architecture and castles, and is one of the best-preserved cities in the Alps. Salzburg, the home of Mozart, is a musical mecca with concerts held nightly. After a day on the town, he checked into a quaint guesthouse on the outskirts of the city. He was tired and thought tomorrow would be an interesting ride through the Alps.

That night at dinner he thought he noticed the same Brownshirts that followed him in Munich. It really didn't register, for he had a peaceful day touring the countryside. After enjoying a late breakfast, he decided to drive further into the mountains. The roads were narrow and always climbing. The landscape, as everyone said, was "spectacular" and David forgot his camera. He was fascinated and distracted by the beauty and didn't realize that he was being followed by a midsize truck. It then hit home.

"Why are they following me? What do they intend to do? Are they just keeping a watch on me to see if I am going to contact anyone?"

The road was narrow and could just about handle traffic going both ways. There were guardrails that hardly seemed sturdy enough to stop you from going over. David wanted to turn around and head back but could not find an opportunity to reverse direction. They were now following extremely close and did not try to hide their mission to trail him. They were pushing him to drive faster, making the turns not only difficult but dangerous.

"Who are these people? What the hell do they want from me?"

This was becoming a very bad dream. What broke his sequence of thoughts was when the truck deliberately drove into the back of his vehicle. David could control the Mercedes, but it was difficult. He had a convertible, and he finally could see the outline of the Brownshirts. Perspiration was forming on his forehead as he fought to keep the car from going out of control. Fear had crept into every inch of his body as he tried to keep from panicking. He gripped the wheel with all his strength to keep in control. There wasn't any traffic flowing toward him to flag down or stop. He was alone, and he tried to hold back the fear.

They smashed into him again and he almost lost control.

"These German bastards are out to kill me because I am a Jew."

Every time the truck rammed into the car, control became more precarious. They were winning. The convertible was taking a beating, and his options were not good.

"I could stop and fight them, but can I hold my own and then outrun them? The road is narrow, and I am at a disadvantage. I can't outrun them. They will run me down."

David felt it was only a matter of time before they would push him off the road to fall seven hundred to eight hundred feet to the valley below. If only he had a weapon—a tire iron or something. "Why isn't there any traffic?"

He had one hand on the wheel and stretched out to search the glove compartment. There was only a flashlight.

"Well, it's better than nothing. At least I have something besides my fists. Maybe there's a tire iron or some piece of metal in the trunk. If I stop, I can possibly get to the trunk before they can reach me."

They continued to smash into the Mercedes. He could tell the convertible was taking a beating. The steering was becoming more erratic by the second. It was decision time. Fight them and possibly see an oncoming car or get sent over the edge.

David slammed on the brakes and the truck careened into the car, pushing it close to the edge. He jumped out and dashed to open the trunk. As he reached for the handle, a tremendous blow struck him. The Brownshirts were just as agile as him. They pounded him with their clubs. David fought back with his flashlight but to no avail. The blows were too well-placed and were coming at a pace he could not stop. He was losing, and consciousness was fading away.

"I am going to die, not seeing my son and daughter grown. I will have lost my beloved Hannah."

All he could think of was what would happen to Hannah and the children. How would they survive?

The Brownshirts continued beating him until there wasn't any movement on David's part. They had done their work, picking him up and placing him behind the wheel. It had to look like an accident. They removed a segment of the railing and pushed the vehicle over the edge. It would fall to the valley floor and, more than likely, explode.

The Mercedes slowly started to slide down the mountainside and then suddenly stopped. It had caught itself on a stunted tree and many vines that had tangled around the chassis. It was now anchored to the tree and the brush, hanging in midair. The Brownshirts could not believe the situation. The car was too far down the mountain for them to reach easily, and it was dangerous. They did not know what to do and decided to leave as quickly as possible to avoid being seen.

David had died from the beating, which went on even after he was unconscious. His mangled body was still intact as the Mercedes dangled over the side of the mountain. The only thing noticeable from the road was a broken railing.

The following morning a road maintenance crew came by, saw the railing, and stopped. They quickly saw the accident and called for a crane to retrieve the wreckage. The body was discovered. David was easily identified, for he had all his papers with him, including his wallet. The American consulate was called in and a full investigation was conducted, to no avail. Siemens and Kruger, David's company, handled the expenses and paperwork to bring David's body back to the States.

The shock to Hannah was unimaginable. Her world was shattered. Her lover, friend, and husband was gone in a moment. How could she go on? She had a five-year-old daughter and a newborn son not eight weeks old. She wanted to die and would have taken her life if it were not for the children. Her grief was beyond description. She was alone. There were only David's parents, who tried to console her. Anna and Karl stayed with Hannah for two weeks, wanting her to come to Iowa. Hannah thanked them for the offer. She needed time to think and caress her children. Her family was in Egypt and unable to come or to help. The world had changed, and everywhere the air was filled with the fear of war.

Chapter Four

The Kruger Company and Siemens put together a financial settlement that amounted to more than two year's salary. They chalked it up to public relations. The press had blasted the whole situation, coming down hard on the company for doing business with the Nazis. The funeral drew a huge crowd, with David's rabbi giving a eulogy that brought tears to the gathering. It was not just the death or the way he died; it was why he died. He was a Jew. As you put it into perspective, it was only the beginning.

Hannah did not have real bonds with the Chicago area. She only had a few friends, mostly parents of Rachel's classmates. She was alone, desperately alone. Hannah had a friend she had known from her university days in the UK. They had kept in touch through the years, for she had married an American and moved to Boston. Catherine was a few years older than Hannah and married a college professor who was on sabbatical. Hannah wanted a change and escape from Chicago. Her connection with David's company only caused her constant pain, and Catherine had come to the funeral and they discussed a possible move to Boston. She knew she would need to work, and her talents in art and art education would be a good fit for employment in the Boston academic and cultural areas.

Catherine sat with her. "Hannah, we need to get you situated in Boston. You can bring the children and stay with us. We have enough room, so it will not be a problem. I can take you on a tour, but you should consider living west of Boston where there is a significant Jewish population and great schools. There is opportunity for you here for a good life for you and the children."

Within three months Hannah was ready to start a life in the Boston area. She and the kids moved to Brookline on the Brighton line and had a good-sized apartment. Rachel was five and ready to go to kindergarten. Michael was six months and growing into a real person. Hannah wanted the children to know their heritage and be able to speak several languages. Arabic was her mother tongue, and as her parents had spoken it to her, she did the same with both of them. She alternated speaking to them in both dialects of Arabic. It was just habit in her parents' house, for they would just alternate daily between the two dialects, Egyptian and Iraqi. There were always family businesspeople in the house from Baghdad.

Hannah poured all her love into Michael, for he was part of David and it kept him alive. She saw him when she looked at her baby. It gave her strength to go on. The move to the Boston area was working out, for she secured a position at the Boston Museum of Fine Arts as one of the assistants to the head of the Egyptology section. The museum was developing one of the finest collections of Egyptian artifacts and was pleased to Have Hannah's expertise. Her knowledge of the systems and procedures enabled the museum to develop formal agreements with the Egyptian government. Life had fallen into place—at least the basics: children, home, work, school. She was coping with life on the outside. Inside, she was trying to quell the great hurt from David's death.

Michael's first memories were vivid pictures of the 1938 hurricane. His nose was pressed up against the glass, mesmerized by falling trees as the wind rattled the windows. Rachel pulled him away. He was two and a half. At three, in his Dr. Denton pajamas, he would jump up and down on the bed, using it as a trampoline. He remembered being five years old and starting kindergarten. Although he spoke English, he wondered why everyone didn't speak the same language as they spoke at home. His second-grade teacher, Miss Scully, used to hit you if you didn't read well, and Sunday School was sometimes fun, for he liked the biblical stories. On December 7, 1941, he was standing in his room putting his crayons and pencils away when the family heard the news on the radio. He started to draw war pictures as his mother was crying.

He really didn't realize he didn't have a father until he reached the age of five or six. The concept didn't register and, even then, it was not really penetrating. He was a big kid for his age, and sports—especially football and basketball—were his favorites. When he came down with the mumps, he was heartbroken that he had to miss his "crucial" basketball game at the YMHA.

At nine years of age, he found out what anti-Semitism was, even though he lived in a quasi-Jewish neighborhood. Hannah was hysterical when he came home one day after school with a bloody nose from an Irish bully. It brought back those black days that were always there in her psyche. At ten, he had a morning paper route that showed him his first lessons of the world: responsibility and how to handle yourself. He became aware of the world, sometimes learning the cold facts.

Not consciously, he wanted a dad. The Jewish bachelor next door and his friend's father, who took him to ball games, seemed to fill some of the void.

He heard the story of his father's death, and it took on a greater importance because now the war had special meaning. He would not go to bed until he heard the latest war reports every evening, and he hated the Germans. It had almost become an obsession.

Rachel was four and a half years older than him and was the perfect sister. Blossoming into a beautiful child, she would become, as her mother, a beauty with dark, piercing features that captivated you almost immediately. She did not remember her dad but became, as Michael, a Nazi-hater in every way.

Hannah was now in her late thirties and only focused on the lives of her children. She advanced at the museum, becoming assistant to the head of the department. Her parents were gone; the war had shattered their lives, their business, their very existence. The whole family and its assets were destroyed. She had no way of finding out what happened to her sister and brother.

They lived on a tight budget. Although Hannah had a full-time position, she earned a limited amount of money. One did not receive a significant salary working in museums and the arts. They got by, just making it. Michael brought his paper route earnings home every week. Rachel babysat twice a week. They found a way to live an "almost middle-class" life.

Hannah was a vibrant, stunning woman, and men were more than interested in her. She had a relationship with a professor at Harvard who was the department head for Middle Eastern studies. He spoke Arabic, and it gave her a sense of her old life with family and friends. It went on for some time and was thought to be blossoming into something more. It never happened, for their religions got in the way. Hannah was a Jew, and if she would remarry, it could only be with a Jew. The relationship ended and both parties went on with their lives.

Michael was always playing football on teams where the players were two or more years older than him. In order to play at the level of competition he wanted, he went to an adjacent neighborhood, Brighton, that bordered Brookline. This was a tough area made up of Irishmen and Italians. He learned to protect himself. Anti-Semitism was flagrant, and although his name did not have a Jewish connotation, he made sure they knew he was a Jew. He inherited that stand-up attitude from his dad. He hung out with this group mainly because of their athletic ability and their common interest in sports. The bond was also brought about by their financial status. They came from hardworking families who struggled to make ends meet.

During the war, they collected scrap metal for the war effort. Near their ballfield was a very large home, more or less out of place in the neighborhood. The "mansion," as he called it, had a huge driveway with wrought-iron fences. The old man he believed was the owner used to scream and throw stones at anyone who would cut through the property to the ballfield. He started cursing Michael and his crew and, for some reason, called them "dirty Jews." There was a fire steaming in Michael, and one night he led the group to rip down the iron fence; not just the gate but twenty to thirty feet of iron, which they brought to the scrap drive. He was the Jewish leader over his Italian and Irish fellow friends and athletes.

His bar mitzvah would be coming, and he attended Hebrew High School four days a week after elementary school. Because of his Arabic language skills, he became almost fluent in Hebrew over-night. Hannah had a very modest party for him. He performed well, but his religious days were over. Sport was his passion, and he was learning about girls.

He gravitated toward his Italian friends and dressed in pegged pants. They were wool and his only dress slacks as he sweated in the heat. The first dance at the Jewish Community Center was somewhat of a disaster. Most of the girls came from wealthy homes. They looked at Michael as if he came from Mars, snickering and laughing. They wanted beaus to be wearing white bucks, chinos, and a blue blazer. He was embarrassed and, from that day forward, swore he would be a fashion plate. The only suit he had was what Hannah had bought him from Robert Hall for his bar mitzvah. He now started to bulge out of it.

When he went to high school, his peers from the better side of town looked at him the same way the girls did at the dance. It took little time for their attitudes to change when he became a starting end on the varsity. His acceptance went to the next level when he was on the starting five of a league-leading basketball squad. It all happened so fast. At his first gym class, the basketball coach told him to be ready to play for the varsity. He was sought after by the school fraternities.

Michael also loved to draw. It was his calling. He could not remember when he did not have a sketch pad in front of him, for this natural talent seemed to grow when he started taking art classes in high school.

His mother and sister were supporting him. He was playing sports instead of working after school. Michael felt he was not pulling his weight. He started moonlighting by washing dishes at a local restaurant in the evenings. Michael was burning the candle at both ends, and it could not go on. Hannah had wanted Michael to play, and she knew David would have been so proud of his son. She took a second job working in a bookstore in Brookline.

Michael found a summer job as a stock boy in a men's and women's fashion clothing store and was totally captivated by the business. The owners could see he had a style sense and design ability, and they pushed him to use his artistic ability to start designing. He learned how to "dress" windows and was doing most of the fashion window and in-store displays by the time school rolled around. He worked whenever he had the time—Saturday in the store and some Sundays in the stockroom. The owners, Abe and Sarah Stone, were childless and more or less "adopted" him. They took him to local vendor shows where they bought the goods for the coming season. The learning experience was second to none. From Robert Hall suits, he began dressing in the latest fashion. Everything was at cost for him and his family. He had found his place and continued to learn about the many areas of the business until he was ready for his college education.

Michael had stopped playing all sports in his senior year and spent whatever time he had working in the store. He learned how to buy and how to manage the inventory. He was schooled in fashion and expanded his design ability. He applied and was accepted to the Rhode Island School of Design. It was his choice, for he wanted to also take courses at Brown. His art portfolio was extremely well-done. His letters of recommendation and résumé gave him high marks. The director of the Boston Museum, where Hannah worked, gave him a glowing recommendation.

Rachel was almost five years older and had just finished her undergraduate program at Northeastern University. She was in a nursing program, wanting to achieve a master's degree. Her ultimate goal was possibly to go to medical school. She was undecided.

Michael looked up to his sister, for she took care of him many a time while Hannah worked evenings in the bookstore. They had an inseparable relationship and confided in one another as they grew to adulthood. Michael felt he had a responsibility to make sure she fulfilled her dreams. He was planning to finance medical school if she so desired.

Brown wanted him to be "their" student and take courses at RISD. They tried to entice him to play football, basketball, or both. Michael did not want to play at the collegiate level. When he had the time, he felt it was better spent in the stores. The coaches just came to the conclusion, "What a waste of talent!"

He was off to Providence, Rhode Island. Hannah was ecstatic Michael was only thirty-five miles away. She could see him at will. He could come home for a meal or to do his laundry. It was less than an hour by train or bus. Michael was in constant touch with his "adoptive" mother and father, who were trying to orchestrate his education along with Hannah. He earned extra money by tutoring students from the Middle East, mainly the Emirates, who were either at Brown or RISD. His proficiency in both dialects was his meal ticket. It was rather interesting—a Jew helping an Arab who swore death to Israel! His interest in Israel was almost to a point of fanaticism.

There were some heart-wrenching times for Michael in his initial year at RISD.. He fell in love with his high school sweetheart, who was a year younger than him and was enrolled in a commercial program, not the college preparatory classes that he attended. Shirley came from a hardworking family. Her father owned a gas station. He fell head over heels for Shirley Arons, and she felt the same way about him. They were inseparable, making plans for a life together. Her parents seemed to like him.

Mrs. Arons said, "Michael, you would never not have food on the table, for you are a go-getter."

When her parents would go away on some weekends, they started sleeping together. Michael was at RISD and came home on weekends to work at the clothing store and see Shirley. One of the many reasons he chose RISD was because he could work at the store and see her, as Brookline was only an hour away.

His world started to change. Shirley started dating a local lawyer who was eight years older. He was tall, handsome, well-established, successful, and from a prominent Jewish family. Michael was heartbroken. She told him she couldn't take a chance with him, for Sam had it all and she did not want to miss out. Michael took it extremely hard, and it affected everything in his life. His grades suffered and his overall attitude became negative. His salvation was his artwork, and he fucked himself nearly to exhaustion with as many coeds as he could muster. Slowly, he came out of his self-induced coma-like attitude. He vowed he would never be put in this position again.

From an early age, he was told the stories of his family in Egypt. Hannah never let him forget where his heritage came from. She always related the history of the family in Arabic, in both dialects, and gave him more than just a snapshot of Egypt—her childhood and her impressions of the country. Michael became totally enamored with anything Egyptian and became an Egyptian history buff. His major interests were the events leading up to World War II and the rise of Egyptian nationalism. He read everything he could get his hands on and just soaked up the facts and events.

His feelings toward Germany were incensed upon reading of the Nazi involvement. Hannah had given him a blow-by-blow account of his father's death. He read about Mussolini launching Italian troops and British-held Egypt and the arrival of Deutsches Afrika Korps commanded by Rommel. Within thirty days the entire Italian-Egyptian force was decimated and thousands were taken prisoners. Weeks later, troops under Rommel arrived and turned the tide. They mounted victories in the desert and outfought the British forces onto Egyptian soil. Rommel's offensive was eventually stopped at El Alamein, just 150 miles from Cairo. His demise was mainly due to the length of his supply lines. The British had the advantage with supplies and fresh troops on hand. With British forces from Malta, Montgomery could stop the advance and force them to retreat westward to Libya and Tunisia.

The Germans' strategic goal was to slice through Egypt, capture the Suez Canal, enter Palestine, start an Arab uprising against the British, and link up with German forces coming from southern Russia. All of this changed with the defeat at El Alamein. Eventually, after several battles pitting Montgomery versus Rommel, the Allies, with the American Eighth Army, finally drove the Desert Fox to withdraw, leaving thirty thousand German troops to surrender.

Winston Churchill's words summed up the events: "Now this is not the end. It is not even the beginning of the end. But it is, perhaps, the end of the beginning."

Michael's artwork had a unique style, and his fashion design was coming from his experiences at retail. Some of his designs were now being produced. Abe and Sarah took his sketches and, with minor corrections, created a line called "Michael Janssen." It was only a few pieces, but they were interesting. More than that, they sold! Michael was ecstatic and living his dream.

Abe and Sarah had not just developed a local fashion store; they were entrepreneurs and expanded the operation in key fashion markets such as New York, Dallas, Los Angeles, and San Francisco. They were highly successful and had a unique approach to fashion. Abe was the businessman and Sarah had the fashion touch. She was grooming Michael to be the fashion director. Sarah had recognized his talent and started his apprenticeship in his junior year in high school. By the time he was at RISD, he was well along in his education.

Chapter Five

Michael still spent many a weekend back in Brookline working with Abe and Sarah and seeing his mother. After a year in the dorms, he found a small apartment on Lloyd Avenue, close to both RISD and Brown. It had great light, for it was on the third floor and had a skylight. He went about making it his home. Using his ingenuity, he made a drawing table with the largest piece of wood he could drag up the stairs. Finding two wooden horses and working on the wood surface with a sander produced exactly what he wanted. The lighting came next, with two gooseneck lamps. The best part was the small terrace that allowed him to sit in the sun. Posters were now placed on the walls. He found Van Gogh prints that brightened the whole room. The apartment started to have the look he wanted, and the ruby red couch and chair he found in a secondhand furniture mart made it all come together. The centerpiece was the king-size bed that served as a major factor in seducing the parade of coeds and some townies finding their way to his "hideaway." Life was good.

In his senior year, Michael decided to take additional courses at Brown in advanced economics and finance. Between the design courses at RISD and the load at Brown, he wanted to assure that he could have enough credits for an MBA program. Michael had his dream of combining his design ability with business smarts to see where it could take him. He had set the bar very high. All he knew was that he had a chance, an opportunity to achieve whatever goals were in his grasp. He wanted it for himself, for his mother and sister, and for his people. His application to graduate school covered all the bases. The combination of his design and scholastic ability set him apart from most of the candidates vying to attend the top schools.

He truly was blessed, receiving acceptances from Stanford and Harvard Business School, among others. Michael was about to make a decision that was the most difficult decision of his life. He wanted to hear Hannah's opinion as well as that of Abe and Sarah, who had played such an important part in his life. They were asked for their thoughts, as they were considered part of his family and his future. He searched out his professors at both institutions for their advice. Michael was torn between the choices, for both offered tremendous advantages.

The decision was Harvard. There was the geographical issue, as it was twenty minutes from Brookline. He wanted to be near Hannah because, in his estimation, she needed him. The real story was that Michael needed the family connection! What turned out to be the tipping point was his relationship with Abe and Sarah. They had grown their business into a fifty-store chain and a very substantial wholesale company. It not only had an established ready-to-wear brand but a growing accessory business, including shoes and hand-bags. They were now major players in the fashion market, starting to develop international retail locations. They were grooming Michael to carry on. Michael was a natural. They had started his education early, and he had the "gift," that fashion sense, in his genes. Cambridge was around the corner from Brookline, just across the Charles River, but really a million miles away. What awaited him was a whole new world. He wanted to get his MBA from Harvard and, at the same time, get a PhD from his mentors who were tutoring him to be the driving force in the business. Both had equal importance, and Michael realized that the combination of the two would bring him everything he wanted.

His social life left nothing to be desired. He was sought after in every way, living in the Back Bay off Commonwealth Avenue in the heart of Boston. Money was not a major issue. Michael was now on the payroll. Abe and Sarah believed that Michael had the ability and drive to lead the business. His education at Harvard, coupled with the opportunity to grow in the business at the same time, was working. His contribution was limited because of his studies, but it was definitely a factor in the growth of the business.

This business was driven by knowing what women wanted, and not only on their backs and feet. To be successful, you not only had to have a great style sense, but you also had to understand what made them tick. Michael had that ability and had that "touch." It could not be taught or acquired at Harvard, for it was part of his genes. Abe and Sarah recognized this in him and gave him every opportunity to mature and grow.

Michael had a lot going on at the same time. Women were everywhere, and all the buyers and executives were women. They performed best and were more than willing to go that extra mile, knowing that the company appreciated them, for he knew how to work with them. Harvard gave him a distinct perspective of the business world. His professors more than welcomed his fashion and retail experience as they discussed case studies.

There were decisions to be made as he was finishing his MBA. Michael had come a long way in a short time. How could he thank his "adoptive" parents for giving him the opportunity of a lifetime? They loved him as the son they never had and were his benefactors. It became a Friday night ritual to all have dinner together, including Hannah and Rachel. Hannah would light the Sabbath candles. They were a family of five with a variety of interests, ideas, and cultural differences. But they were one family in the eyes of each other.

There had been six years of schooling in every conceivable manner. The summers were filled with working in the business. He was doing double duty between Harvard and the stores. He wanted a break, some time away from the academics and even his education in the business. There wasn't any question that he enjoyed the intrigue, adventure, and excitement of the fashion world, but a change and break was needed. Six months away from everything was the plan. Michael had never taken a vacation. When he was a child, the family went to Cape Cod for three days. Time was what he needed—a complete change away from the books and away from the retail business. His massive workload these past years necessitated refueling of the body, mind, and spirit. A six-month hiatus was what he was thinking.

He sat down with Abe and Sarah. "I just want you to know how much I appreciate everything that you have done for me. I would not be involved with what I love doing without you giving me the opportunity to learn the business. You are as close to me as my mother and have opened doors I would never have discovered. My game plan worked by going to Harvard Business School and working with you through that period. This is where I want to be. The learning experience at Harvard will give me all the tools to help the business. It wasn't easy being pulled in two directions, the business and Harvard. But it is the road that I have chosen, and I know you will support me."

Abe looked at him. "We want you to succeed more than you will ever know. You can take this business to the next level. You have all the qualifications. All we ask is that you be honest and loyal. We want to spoil your future children."

He really hadn't put much thought into what he wanted to do during this six-month hiatus. What would he like? Where would he want to go? The lightbulb went on, and it was Israel.

It was always Israel. Where else would he go? It was his magical place—the land of milk and honey, the land of all the stories of his childhood.

Hannah had read him countless biblical tales, and he recited them in Hebrew and Arabic. His mother had learned them in Hebrew from her father and felt it was about their homeland and they should be told in that tongue. It was time to live his dream. Michael had this close connection with Israel since childhood. His father had challenged the Nazis because he was a Jew, and it cost him his life. The ties between his father and Judaism and Israel were inseparable and sacred to him. Being there would give him the opportunity to know the country, the people, and the history.

He wanted to know what made these people tick. How did they live every day with enemies all around them? Why were they winning against the entire Arab world?

Michael was ready for the journey and realized he could come back a different person. He didn't realize the experience would be the most significant of his young life. Michael had read volumes about the country, and he wanted to see every inch of it. It was 1957, and to understand what was happening, you had to go back to see what occurred before and after Israeli independence in 1948. Michael ran his memory tapes of Israel's creation. It was only nine years since the birth of the Israeli State. After the partition of Palestine into one Jewish and one Arab state in 1947, there was widespread fighting. The Jewish communities were attacked. It was clear the Arab world's purpose was to destroy them. When Britain left, the Jewish and Arab militias jockeyed for position in anticipation of the Arab invasion. Hoping to escape the strife, there was an Arab exodus before the war started. It was presumed there would be a victory and they would return to their homes. Approximately 175,000 Arabs left Palestine.

On May 14, 1948, Israel was proclaimed a republic, and the next day the joint armies of Egypt, Jordan, Syria, Lebanon, and Iraq invaded. The Arab forces were far superior in number but lacked coordination. There was internal strife between the Arab government, which caused their demise. On the other hand, the Israelis, although a smaller force and not as well-equipped, used their organizational skills and nationalistic spirit to turn the tide. When the final ceasefire came in the spring of 1949, the Israelis controlled 40 percent more land than the proposed UN partition plan. Egypt and Jordan occupied the Gaza Strip and the West Bank.

During the fighting, many Palestinian Arabs fled or were driven from the areas that came under Israeli control. Around 300,000 fled to the neighboring Arab countries while approximately 420,000 ended up in refugee camps in the occupied part of Palestine. How many fled out of fear of the advancing Israeli forces is questionable. Many Arabs were forced from their homes by Israeli troops. What the true numbers were was a matter of interpretation on both sides. The Egyptians and Jordanians still controlled certain areas, including the old city of Jerusalem.

From the moment Israel was created in 1948, the door was opened for the hundreds of thousands of Jewish refugees who had survived the Holocaust. At the same time, Jews in Arab countries found themselves subject to violence and persecution. Israel launched a program to evacuate the Jews of Yemen and Iraq. The Syrian and Lebanese Jews fled to Israel. There was another exodus from Egypt, Tunisia, Algeria, Libya, Morocco, Iran, and Turkey. A total of about 650,000 refugees came from Muslim countries to Israel. The Arab countries, with their far greater capacity for absorption, did not integrate the roughly 720,000 Palestinian Arab refugees. They were strictly confined to refugee camps and used as political tools in the ongoing fight with Israel.

In the 1950s, Egypt took over Jordan's role as the sponsor of terror against Israel, specifically from Gaza. The Egyptian naval blockade denied Israeli shipping through the Suez Canal. The blockade was expanded to include the passage of all foreign ships to the Red Sea port of Eilat. From 1949 to 1956, the armed truce between Israel and the Arabs, enforced in part by the UN forces, was inundated with raids and reprisals. The world powers—the United States, Great Britain, and France—sided with Israel while Russia supported Arab demands. A number of events occurred in the 1950s that placed Israel in a permanent position of war and severe danger.

In the beginning of 1949, the Soviet Union turned from one of Israel's only allies into one of its staunchest enemies. Much of it had to do with Russia's hope for a Communist government with Israel, which never materialized. Stalin's latent anti-Semitism began to surface and was a major reason for Russia changing its position. They joined the Arabs in a common cause, and anti-Semitism played a major role. There was an additional setback when the UN voted that Jerusalem should be an international city run by the United Nations. The playing field was changing and a whole new scenario was developing in Egypt. King Farouk was deposed. The military staged the revolution, and the man who really was behind it was Abdel Nasser.

Nasser was a dominant figure, not only in Egypt but in the Arab world. He was born in Alexandria and lost his mother when he was six years old. He found the path to success at an early age when politics came into his life. In 1935 Nasser became part of the revolutionary movement calling for the reinstallation of a constitution for independence. His efforts helped establish the Egyptian Nationalist Movement in 1936. He joined the army and became an officer, graduating from the military academy in 1938, spending time in the Sudan. At the end of 1944, Rommel was driving toward the western territory of Egypt. Nasser was assigned to a British battalion near El Alamein.

The British forced King Farouk to abdicate in 1942. Nasser was promoted to captain and was an instructor at the academy. He and his wife helped form the Free Officers Movement, which had a key role in the revolution and future events. When Palestine was divided in 1947, the officers sided with the Arab States to oppose Israel. He was disgusted with the graft, lack of organization, and self-interest that allowed the Israelis to defeat the Egyptian forces in 1949. He suffered wounds and was awarded the Military Star Medal for distinguished service. In 1951 Nasser became a major, secretly organizing the Free Officers' commandos against the British forces in the Suez Canal region. The military staged a revolution, but Nasser was really the force behind it. There was a power play on his part that culminated in his heading the Revolution Council, which resulted in him being elected president in 1956.

Tensions mounted during 1956 as Israel became convinced that the Arabs were preparing for war. The nationalization of the Suez Canal by Nasser in July 1956 resulted in the further alienation of Great Britain and France, who made new agreements with Israel.

On October 29, 1956, Israeli forces, directed by Moshe Dayan, launched a combined air and ground assault into Egypt's Sinai Peninsula. Early Israeli successes were reinforced by an Anglo-French invasion along the Suez Canal. Although the action against Egypt was severely condemned by the nations of the world, the ceasefire of November 6, was endorsed by the United Nations. Support came from the United States and Soviets only after Israel captured several key objectives, including the Gaza Strip and Sharm El Sheikh, which commanded the approaches to the Gulf of Aqaba. Without this access, Israel was cut off from the Indian Ocean. They were now guaranteed access. On March 16, 1957, under unrelenting pressure from the United States, Israel withdrew from all the territory it had occupied in the Sinai Peninsula during the invasion of Egypt less than five months earlier. Israel's insistence on keeping a military presence in parts of the Sinai led to tense relations between President Eisenhower and Prime Minster David Ben Gurion. From the very beginning of what became known as the Suez Crisis, Eisenhower had opposed the secret plot by Britain, France, and Israel to invade Egypt. He had managed to stop the invasion but not before the Israeli troops occupied Egypt's Sinai Peninsula with Moshe Dayan commanding the operation. Britain and France bowed to Eisenhower's request and removed their troops. They had won their objective by keeping the canal open. Despite repeated US urging, Ben Gurion refused to withdraw Israeli troops. Eisenhower put immense pressure on Israel to comply and went to the UN asking for Israel to withdraw.

Chapter Six

THIS WAS THE ISRAEL THAT MICHAEL SAW WHEN HE arrived in the summer of 1959. He sensed he was a totally different person when he stepped off the plane, his white linen shirt opened at the neck, showing off the tan that was so easy to acquire because of his sandy skin color. His deep, penetrating eyes were forever surveying the immediate world. His body was sculpted from continuous workouts at the university facilities. He was beautiful, handsome, whatever adjective you wanted to use. Most women would not miss the chance of taking a second look as he strode by.

His association with his adoptive parents gave him the opportunity to wear the latest fashion apparel. Being involved with fashion couture and better product gave him a unique perspective regarding women. Not only did he learn how to dress them, and at times undress them, he understood their personalities and their attitudes toward not only fashion but how they approached issues. It was a great advantage in business as well as life. His sophistication was way beyond his years.

These were the skills he acquired throughout his experiences and education. He was about to see a new world, one that he anticipated his whole life. He knew the history and the problems facing this new nation. What he did not know was how they were going to affect him. The custom doors opened, and there was his friend from Brown and Harvard. Bengy was there to greet him. "Shalom, my friend."

Benjamin Barak was older than Michael, for he had spent three years in the compulsory military services as all Israeli males do. Even women had to serve two years of the same. Bengy and Michael had developed a great friendship over their years at Brown and Harvard. Michael's proficiency in Arabic translated to an easy pickup of Hebrew, in which he had a basis from his childhood schooling. They were very close, and Michael confided in him. He was like a big brother and understood what made Michael tick. Bengy knew the story of his dad and his almost fanatical attitude toward anything to do with the German participation in World War II.

They were very similar in their likes and dislikes. Bengy, as Michael, was a man's man: tall, bronze blondish hair, blue eyes. He had the typical Nordic features and stature. He spoke English without a trace of an accent and knew all the nuances of the language. He was born in Israel, better known as a Sabra, and his world centered around his people and country.

Bengy wasn't an ordinary soldier. In fact, he was not a soldier at all. He had been recruited out of Hebrew University for his overall skills in almost anything he touched. He was one of those unique human beings who excelled in any endeavor once he put his mind to it. Bengy had taken an entire battery of psychological tests and been administered an exhausting physical exam by his recruiters. Israel wanted him badly.

The Mossad is the national intelligence agency of Israel. It literally means the "Institute" and is short for Ha Mossad LeModi in ule Tafkidim, which means Institute for Intelligence and Special Operations. It is one of the main entities in the Israeli Intelligence

Community, along with A'man, Military Intelligence, and Shin Bet, internal security. Mossad is responsible for intelligence collection, covert operations, and counterterrorism. It is responsible for protecting Jewish communities and bringing Jews to Israel when official agencies are forbidden to do so. It was formed in 1949 by Prime Minster Ben Gurion, who wanted to coordinate all three segments of the security organization and have them report directly to him.

"So you are finally here! We've talked about it over the past years we've known each other, and I thought about you coming a hundred times, and now it's a reality!"

"Michael, you are about to get a whole different education. Israel is a different way of life than living in Boston. We are, in a sense, what America was a hundred years ago. We are building a nation, a way forward for our people. As Americans, you come from all over the globe but with one common goal. We are the same. As Jews, we want peace, freedom, and the right to grow with our hopes and desires. It is not an easy life in many aspects, but it is our land and we shall make it our home for all the generations to come. Let's get you started. It's been a long journey, and you must be tired. We will start your introduction to Israel tomorrow."

"It has always been my dream to be here. I want you to know this trip is really important to me. Yes, I want a vacation, but I want and need to see my heritage and its people."

Bengy became his tour guide, taking to the task with full enthusiasm. Michael was staying with him in Jerusalem, which would be the first stop on the itinerary. He had a good working history of the origins of Jerusalem. He ran his memory tapes and remembered it was called the City of David and settled in the millennium BCE 6. In 1538 walls were built to define the old city. Today it is divided into four quarters—American, Christian, Jewish, and Muslim. There were a hundred facts in his head, and he wanted them to come to life throughout his stay in Israel. They toured every corner of the city and devoured its contents from Vad Yashem to the falafel stands on Ben Yahuda Street.

Bengy had other plans for Michael. He realized he was not only brilliant but had this burning desire not only to help both Israel and the Jewish people but to cast a blow against the tyranny that took his father's life. He was the perfect candidate for the Mossad to develop and use in its operations in Egypt and Iraq. Michael had all the tools, for he was totally fluent in the dialects and looked the part. He was American, which could be a problem as well as an asset, but Bengy felt Michael's overwhelming desire to help wherever he could would not get in the way. Nothing was certain, but he thought he would be the perfect candidate to work with his people for Israel, for justice.

"Let's go to dinner tonight with some of my friends you haven't met yet. They are pretty interesting people in every way. They are from Tel Aviv, so let's go enjoy one of the great restaurants there."

Tel Aviv was founded in 1909 by sixty Jewish immigrants on the outskirts of the ancient port city of Jaffa. The two entities merged in 1950 with its nickname, the White City. The city was full of life in direct contrast to Jerusalem, more secular and the heart of the developing business community. It was also the home of the Mossad, and they were always looking for that person who could bring them an advantage in the never-ending game of keeping Israel safe.

"So here are my friends, Aron Harel and Joshua Zamir."

"So how are you getting along with this guy? It's one thing to put up with him at Harvard, but here in Israel he probably is more of an asshole!"

51

Michael chuckled. "I think you have hit the nail on the head. I had to carry him for six years at Brown and Harvard, and now he's trying to get back at me, dragging me around Jerusalem day and night."

Aron laughed and said, "So tell us who the hell you are" as Joshua pushed another beer in front of Michael.

"I guess I'm just a 'yokel' trying to find my way in this wonderful country. It has been a real eye-opener to see what this phenomenon is all about. I haven't seen a lot of it, as this jerk"—he pointed to Bengy—"has run my ass off just in Jerusalem."

Aron was smiling. "Well, you will, and must see the country in every aspect. We, as Sabras, are living the dream every day. We strive to build Israel into a haven for all those who wish and need to come to a friendly shore. We feel as a country we have the opportunity to build Israel into a first-class nation. We know our assets and liabilities and what our mission is to our people and heritage. We are more than aware of what we are up against in living among our neighbors. Unfortunately, the surrounding climate is, shall we say, confrontational. It demands a dedication for some of us to give our time and, in some instances, our lives to keep Israel safe and the dream of a better life in our grasp. Reality must be addressed, and that demands dedication by all of us to do our part."

Bengy chimed in: "You guys are getting really serious, so let's have dinner."

Aron and Joshua were full of questions for Michael. Although they knew Michael's background, they feigned ignorance. Michael gave them almost a blow-by-blow narrative of his history over a series of beers and again emphasized the story of his dad and the account of his death. They discussed the current situation facing

Israel superficially, no specifics. Aron and Joshua were interested in Michael's reaction. Everyone was feeling no pain! The evening, as far as Michael was concerned, was delightful. He had great company and a fun time. He was well aware that both were very interested in his history and his state of mind, more than just interested. Bengy drove back to Jerusalem and Michael kind of dozed. There was not much additional conversation over the events of the evening. That would come later.

The next morning, they made their plans to return to the project at hand. Michael wanted to spend time in the museums. They had just taken a general tour of the city so he could catch the flavor and get his bearings. He wanted to start at Yad Vashem, for it is the official memorial to the victims of the Holocaust. Although his dad had died before the Holocaust, he deeply associated his death with the six million who perished.

The memorial consisted of several complexes: the Children's Memorial, the Hall of Remembrance, and the Museum of Holocaust Art. There were sculptures, a research institute with archives, and an International Center for Holocaust Studies. A core goal of the Yad Vashem was to recognize non-Jews who, at personal risk, chose to save Jews from the genocide. There is a section of Yad Vashem, known as the Garden of the Righteous, that honors those persons. The name Yad Vashem is taken from a verse in the Book of Isaiah: "Even unto them will I give in my home and within my walls a place and a name better than of sons and daughters. I will give them an everlasting name." The entire theme of the memorial was to establish a national depository of the names of Jewish victims who had no one to carry their names after death.

The museum complex had just opened to the public in 1957, and the throngs of visitors were endless. The experience was especially moving for Michael. He identified with every area of the complex. Every moment brought back memories of his dad and empathy for the victims. It was a whirlwind tour covering the country from the Golan to Elat. Bengy brought some of his friends who were involved in the archeological digging to give Michael a complete history of the region. He went to the kibbutzes and spent time speaking with the people working the land. Everything was so exciting, for he was impressed with what had been achieved. He saw how the desert came to life and was lined in green. It was a miracle how it was accomplished.

CHAPTER SEVEN

HIS WORLD HAD EXPANDED, AND WHAT HE WAS SEEING made a lasting impression in every conceivable way. His Judaism and feelings for Israel were one, almost impossible to separate. Bengy had done his part, opening the door for him to see all before him. He had soaked up the culture, the beauty, the determination, and the desire to be part of this great country. All that he stood for was there in front of him. All that he desired was within his reach. All that he wanted to contribute was feasible, regardless of what was involved.

When Bengy was finished with all the tours, museums, archeological digs, and wonderful nights, there were other activities that were intensely interesting. He had to get to know the beautiful women of this country.

As Bengy put it, it was a labor of love, and Michael did not shirk his duty. He showed his willingness to make sure all were satisfied.

Aron and Joshua reappeared, not that they were very far away at any time, watching him, his actions, his enthusiasm, his sincerity, his whole conception of Israel from every viewpoint. They wanted him, they needed him, for he could unlock the doors and see what was happening in Egypt that was so disturbing. They thought he was one of the candidates to fill a missing part of the picture.

They had done their research and found some interesting facts. Hannah's family was still functioning in Cairo. The Mossad had put together a fairly accurate account of what had been the history of Hannah's family. The parents had passed on, and their import-export business had suffered a similar fate. Hannah's mother was able to hold on for a considerable length of time, but with the events of the conflict, all was lost.

Hannah had two siblings and had tried numerous times to reach them to no avail. She had no idea where they were or if they were even alive. The conflict had cut off any possibility to communicate with any reliable source in Egypt. The war was over, but there were events going on that put life for Jews in Egypt in peril. The Middle East had emerged as a sanctuary for Nazis fleeing Europe in the 1950s. It had its roots in the anti-British and pro-Nazi attitudes of Vichy Syria, Rashed, Ali in Iraq, King Farouk of Egypt, and the Grand Mufti in Jerusalem. Egypt became, as Arabia, a safe haven for Nazi experts who escaped the Allied dragnet. They were hired by the king as military, financial, and technical advisors. Large numbers of Nazi fugitives who had escaped to Argentina were given key posts in the new republican regime in Egypt. Former members of the Waffen SS were training the troops of the Egyptian Army. German and Austrian scientists were deployed in the aircraft and missile centers that were built in Egypt. Their goals centered around the destruction of Israel.

In 1948 seventy-five thousand Jews lived in Egypt. In 1956 four thousand were expelled, losing all property rights. One year later, all Jews not in continuous residence since 1900 were deprived of citizenship. It was a nightmare and resembled the history of the 1930s with Germany and Europe.

Aron and Joshua felt it was time to see if Michael was their candidate. They thought he was ready to be approached, and they wanted to tell their story in a way that would not sell him to join them but show him the necessity for him to help his family, his people, his heritage.

The Mossad had recruited Egyptian Jews in 1954 to bomb a series of Egyptian, American, and British civilian targets. Their goal was to create an image of instability to persuade the British to maintain their military occupation of the Suez Canal zone, but the plan failed and forced the resignation of the Israeli defense minister.

They drove Michael out of Jerusalem under the pretense of a lunch in the country. Aron kept needling him on his supposed conquests of the female population. They sparred back and forth, all in fun. They had become friends and truly liked one another. There was a real bond between them. Over the last weeks they had seen one another in different situations and settings from the discos of Tel Aviv to the halls of Yad Vashem.

They had developed a friendship that was based on similar interests that ranged from the serious to fun.

Michael believed there was more to this lunch than a satisfying meal in the country. He was not surprised when the subject became serious and the participants focused the conversation on their reason for being here.

"So, Michael, we have brought you out here not only for a fine lunch but to see if you are willing to help us keep this land of Israel safe from all who wish to destroy us. That's our job: to keep this country from harm. To do this, there are times that we must be on the offensive and strike a blow that will keep danger from our shores. Often it is necessary to send our people into foreign territory to make this happen. That is why we are here talking to you."

"How can I possibly help you? The only thing I am good at is being a fashion person and here in Israel getting Sabras into my bed."

"We know what you're good at. We know you have a skill that we need to make this strategic operation work: your ability to speak two dialects of Arabic perfectly and also to pass as an Egyptian or Iraqi. There is another component: your fashion know-how. You happen to be a perfect fit for what we believe is the key element needed for this operation we are planning. The question is: Are you willing to help us? We know you have a love for this land and its people. I cannot tell you what we are planning. I can only tell you that it will be dangerous and will be necessary to use all the skills we will give you. We are not looking for an answer today. It is probably the most difficult decision you will ever have to make. This is asking a lot from you, for you do not live in Israel. We realize the connection you have to this country and the history of your family. Now, let's eat, and I hope we have not upset your digestion."

There were questions asked by Michael, but mainly he listened. In a sense, it was not real. He actually was not here; this was a dream. He was living a fantastic fantasy, and he could not believe what was happening.

"Am I willing to do this? Am I equipped in my own mind to be able to deliver the results needed? Am I capable of making this happen? Could this be the way to avenge my father's death?"

These thoughts were being tossed around in his psyche as he listened to them. It was too much to consume in one sitting, and they all realized it was time to put the conversation on hold. Michael had to absorb everything that was put forth. It was time not only to rethink what was said but to realize how all this would shape the present and his future.

Michael called his mother early the next morning. It was six a.m. in Jerusalem and ten p.m. in Brookline. She was thrilled to hear from him, and they chatted over what was happening in the family. Rachel had a boyfriend and everything was going well at the museum. Michael did not mention anything about his lunch meeting. He kept the conversation moving with his descriptions of the country and the people. Naturally there were questions on Hannah's part, the basics that a mother asks her son. Michael asked about Abe and Sarah, for they were part of the family. When he hung up, he made a mental note to call them later at their office. He felt relieved, knowing they all were well. But more so, it made him feel that it was his responsibility to make their world safe and secure. Israel was the only place in their sometimes frightening, violent, complex world where his loved ones could be truly safe from oppression. Generations of history had proven the need for a Jewish homeland. The United States was his home, and he was an American, not only in name but in his willingness to do whatever was needed to make it safe for all.

Michael thought it would be best to speak with Abe and Sarah. He wasn't about to tell them what he was debating doing, but they were so important to him that he felt it would be almost sacrilegious not to keep them somewhat in the loop.

"Well, kid, how's it going in the land of milk and honey?"

Michael chuckled. "I guess all is well here. At least it looks that way. These Jews are tough. They have all these 'friendly' states around them just chomping at the bit to take them down. I can't believe how they function under these conditions. What is amazing is how they are growing and flourishing." They discussed business and what was happening back in the States.

"You would be really pleased with the new collection. We had all the merchandisers and managers in to view the collections. Some of the items you developed before leaving had a terrific response from the staff. We feel two or three could be key looks for the season. They were more than impressed. They all send their regards and hope you do not come home exhausted by the Israeli Sabra beauties.

Michael laughed. "I am so happy they liked the new items. I was hoping there was a good response."

"It was an exceptional response. We want you to relax and enjoy Israel, but we need you home. We miss you. I know you have a burning desire to do everything in your power to help them. Just stay out of trouble."

Michael chuckled. "You know I wouldn't even consider landing in that situation."

Abe started to laugh. "My boy, you are talking to me . . . stay safe!"

Chapter Eight

Aron and Joshua knew their customer. The stories of Nazis appearing in Egypt had triggered a response from Michael. He could never forget his father's death at the hands of the Brownshirts. What made the decision impossible to reject was the realization that part of his family still existed in Egypt. The possibility of helping them was in his power.

During their phone conversations, Hannah asked Michael to check the registries of any Egyptian Jews who had recently come to Israel. She always had hope that somehow or another her brother and sister had escaped.

How could he say no? It was his obligation and duty as a Jew, a member of this family, to bring them from harm's way. Michael spent the week in deep thought. He had not been to the synagogue since he arrived in Israel. Not that he was very religious, but he observed the key holidays: Rosh Hashanah, Yom Kippur, and Passover. He went to Friday night services and prayed that what he was about to do would help Israel and his fellow brethren. It was September, and the holidays were coming. The family always went to Temple Israel together. He would celebrate with Bengy, but his heart was in Brookline, Massachusetts. His Hebrew was now fluent, and the chanting of Kol Nidre had taken on a special meaning. Tears were wiped away as he said the Kaddish for his dad.

Michael knew he had made the decision during the long lunch. He just kept debating it with himself, looking for reasons not to do it. The internal debate went on, for he couldn't escape the dilemma. He wanted to be part of the fight for Israel. Was it right for him, as an American, to put himself in harm's way for this country? That argument didn't hold long, for what could develop in Egypt could bring terror to many around the globe.

The holidays seemed to give him added reason to think of all the pros and cons. He didn't have an alternative in his estimation. The die was cast. He was ready to stand up and be counted. He had made the decision on what he thought was the basis of his values.

He did call Abe and Sarah again. After the pleasantries, he told them how he felt about being in Israel, nothing else. When Abe hung up the phone, he remarked to Sarah, "Our boy could be in danger. I sensed it in his voice. He needs our prayers now!"

There was much to be done in a brief time. He had to learn a whole new way of life in many aspects. He was fluent in Arabic but not in the customs or the way an Arab man conducts himself in life's situations. Michael had to learn how to approach this whole life as an Egyptian or as an Iraqi in Egypt. Although he spoke both dialects perfectly, he needed to grasp this lifestyle, at least to understand it. He was supposed to be an Englishman, but he had to know he was still an Arab when necessary.

There was a difference of opinion on the part of the organization on how they should proceed. They had developed two to three scenarios and wanted to see which one would be the best fit for the project. In the meantime, Michael had to learn to be a spy. It was round-the-clock work teaching him every aspect of surveillance, communication, and the use of weapons.

Michael was told everything they knew about Nasser and Israel's involvement in the Suez Canal crisis. It was key, as his knowledge of the events was essential. Things were falling into place. He had a running history of the events and was ready to move on in his education and schooling. He had somewhat of an idea what Egypt was like from the stories Hannah had told of the family. It was part of his life hearing about Cairo, his grandfather and grandmother. It was his mother's interpretation of her life that gave him the confidence to attempt this undertaking. Years of stories about the everyday events made him feel he had, in some way, been there.

Generally, candidates must take a variety of psychological and aptitude tests. Michael did not fall into this category. They had assessed his qualities over a three-month period and found him more than suitable for what they needed. His situation was so unique. He would be part of a Mossad operation but not really an intelligence officer. Michael was not a Katsa, a field agent of the national agency of Israel. He was there because of his ability to fill their special needs. No one else had the credentials to do the work that was needed. Michael did go to their training academy, the Midrasha, located near the town of Herzliya.

The program for applicants to become operatives was a three-year course. His education had to be condensed into a month. They needed action, and the clock was ticking against them. Certain aspects of the educational process had to be completed in full, avoiding car and foot surveillance. There were numerous exercises and many exams in the streets of Jerusalem and Tel Aviv. There was an extensive course on firearms. You could not send an agent into harm's way without these skills. It was a crash course, and Michael found he had an aptitude and skill for handling firearms. He became an accurate marksman in a relatively short time. Shooting at a target and another human being were totally different experiences, to say the least.

The thought was always with him whenever he practiced: "Am I capable of actually killing?"

CHAPTER NINE

THE NAZI CONTINGENT IN EGYPT WAS BECOMING A REAL threat. Farouk had brought scientists and ex-military personnel to develop a full-scale force that would be used against Israel. Now Nasser pushed it to the next level. This was no longer Arabs squabbling and being unorganized among themselves as was the general situation in the past. It was now a German mentality and organization to create a real threat to Israel. They were developing the V-2 rockets in Egypt. The Egyptian Army was being trained by the Waffen SS. There was a whole cast of characters who escaped Europe and settled in either South America or in the Middle East, mainly Cairo and some in Damascus.

The need to know what was occurring was a necessity, and the Mossad was using many methods to gain as much information as possible. The basic plan was to stop the flow of materials and recruits from West Germany and Switzerland that were pouring in to build a whole new military and scientific organization.

The driving force and mastermind planner was Hassan Sayed Streiger, a German-Swiss-Egyptian arms dealer. Born to a German father and Egyptian mother, his father had deep ties to the Third Reich. The connection went back to the early 1930s and helped the Nazi party gain a foothold in the Weimar Republic. As an industrialist, he weathered the fall of Nazi Germany and passed on his chemical business to his son. Hassan's mother came from a very influential Egyptian family. Hassan was trilingual, schooled in Germany and Switzerland, and became a powerful chief executive and owner of a thriving industrial complex. Instead of using these resources to develop a legitimate business, Hassan turned to manufacturing munitions and acting as an agent to supply mainly the Third World with illicit arms. Between his father's political leaning and his Egyptian heritage, he became a major supporter of Nasser and had an agenda that was centered on the destruction of Israel. Hassan's association with Nasser brought millions to his companies.

He was sophisticated in every way and looked the part of a successful international businessperson. Hassan wore custom-made suits, a gold Rolex, and handmade Church footwear. He had Nordic features, with his mother's coloring and salt-and-pepper hair perfectly cut, and at more than six feet tall, he was an imposing figure. Hassan was concerned with his body fitness and worked with a personal trainer most mornings. His organization was composed of Germans, Swiss, and Egyptians. Hassan's right-hand man was Walter Schmidt, an ex-SS lieutenant who had escaped the investigations conducted by the Allies. He was extremely bright and assembled a staff that was loyal to him. His holdings were worldwide; he was a munitions dealer selling his wares to anyone who could pay the price. Hassan's clients included the banana republics of Africa and the revolutionaries of the world. Hassan's main customer was now Egypt, with ties to Nasser, not only as a business relationship but through his wife's family. They were being joined at the hip as Hassan felt that his influence in Egypt would grow—not only the business relationship but also his political ambitions. He was considered an Egyptian citizen because of his mother. He had the means and the opportunity to be perceived as a shining star in Egypt as well as in the Middle East. He was willing to bankroll Nasser in the development of all the facets of a military buildup. His German heritage and schooling gave him the discipline and experience to go about his business and political dealings with the utmost cunning and seriousness.

He maintained two offices, one in Munich and the other in Cairo. His warehousing and development center was in Essen, the heart of the Ruhr Valley and the industrial center of Germany. Munich was the original home of the Nazi Party and still had many sympathizers to the Reich. In his Cairo office, he had free rein of movement in every way. Hassan had to limit his activity in Germany, as he was under constant scrutiny by the West Germans. He had a highly developed worldwide organization for the distribution of his armaments, leasing two air cargo jets to facilitate delivery and distribution. He was a tech fanatic and had spent heavily on a communication system that rivaled the spy networks of the leading powers of the world. It was housed near Cairo and run by the only woman in his organization, Doria Sadat, a brilliant mathematician and communications expert.

Hassan needed cover for his activities, a legitimate business that allowed him to fly cargo in and out of Egypt to the destinations for their sale of weapons. He developed an import/export business in Egyptian cotton sheets and manufactured inexpensive garments that were sold to the Third World. It was a lucrative business that achieved significant margins. Nasser was a champion for women's rights and their place in the workforce, which was one of the reasons Hassan chose Doria Sadat. It was his choice and Nasser's wishes that made it even easier for him to make her the responsible head of this sector of his business.

Doria was an Egyptian beauty—statuesque, with teal blue eyes and olive skin. She carried herself with the grace of a fashion model.

Her parents were academics and had held senior positions at the university in Alexandria. She was educated in that system but spent two years in London to gain her advanced degree. This was quite unusual, and in a way, she had followed the same route as Hannah.

It was a German colony of significant size that had grown in Egypt, led by scientists who were offered positions by the Egyptian government. They were there to develop sophisticated weapon systems based on the same rocket programs they were working on in Germany. The materials had to come from Germany and Switzerland. Although there was an embargo on arms and components in the Middle East, Hassan and company were circumventing the rules. It fell to the Mossad to find a way to stop this development. The key to this was to defeat Hassan and his organization. He was a threat to Israel, and it was now a necessity to find a way to bring him down along with everyone associated with him.

The prime minister gave the marching orders. It was imperative to take care of this situation. The only restraint put on the organization was not to create an international incident. In other words, do not get caught!

Aron and Joshua were the architects of the plan. They had enlisted the help of the entire organization and kicked around many options. They finally came up with what they thought was a well-devised strategy that would achieve the necessary results.

Michael was the key part of the operation. He had no idea how it would play out, but he had signed on without reservation. Everything depended on the ability to penetrate Hassan's organization. This was not an easy task, as the only middle-management employees were German, Swiss, or Egyptian. The rules were straight from Hassan—no deviations!

Chapter Ten

His education was in full swing. Michael was a quick learner and had the gift of memorizing chunks of information easily. It was time to get down to specifics. They brought Michael to an estate outside of Haifa to go over the details. He was brought up to date on all aspects of the operstion by an expert in each field. Joshua and Aro reviewed hisperformance.

First, his cover! Michael's ability to speak two dialects of Arabic flawlessly was a plus. His appearance was perfect for the situation. His knowledge of the fashion business would give him the credentials to develop a cover to penetrate Hassan's organization. Aron and Joshua had labored endlessly on how to insert Michael into the fray. They needed help, and it had to come from the outside.

Sir Arthur Brooks owned the world's largest fashion business. His concept of clothing at a price point for the fashion-conscious working person had resulted in his gaining a significant portion of the contemporary women's and men's markets. His idea of developing the product from the initial sketch to being on the rack was not only brilliant but gave him total control of every step in the process. His organization could bring an idea to fruition at retail in a matter of a few weeks. Fantastique had grown to two thousand stores throughout the world.

Sir Arthur was a Sayan, a Hebrew term that meant "helper," a person willing to work for Israel. He had volunteered as a non-Israeli Jew to help in any way. His parents had fled Russia to escape the pogroms and finally ended up in the UK. As a young man entering the business world, he changed his name from Brotofsky to Brooks. His rise to his position today was one of the great retail and fashion stories, culminating in knighthood. He started out peddling clothing door-to-door and developed a fashion business that brought what was in vogue to the customer at a price.

He was a man of sixty-odd years and as elegant as one could be. Saville Row suits and attire were his trademark. He stood six feet tall; his silver locks were perfectly groomed. He was a handsome man, always bronzed from his favorite escape to St. Bart's and his racing "swan" in Porto Cervo. He never forgot his humble beginning and his desire to help the cause.

Aron and Joshua had set up a meeting with Sir Arthur at a safe house outside London. They needed time with him, which could not be accomplished in his offices behind his flagship store on New Bond Street.

"What can I do for you, gentlemen, that is so urgent as to whisk me away from London?"

"Sir Arthur, we need you to give us a presence in Egypt, principally Cairo."

They laid out the situation, giving him the history of the past year that made this a priority to the State of Israel. They gave Sir Arthur as much information as they could without delving into the needed secrecy. He had to be a partner, for his involvement was critical to the success of the operation. Michael had to become a key player in his organization in order to develop his cover.

"We have to give him a history and a new name. What we would like to accomplish is to insert Daniel Hussein Amin, of Iraqi and Egyptian descent, into your organization."

His historical résumé would be as follows: The family had lived in the UK. They told Sir Arthur their candidate's ability to speak Arabic was vital. Michael, now Mr. Amin, would need an iron-clad history, for he definitely would be vetted in every way. It was a major undertaking, and asking Sir Arthur to undertake this project was asking a lot. Michael would have to spend at least a month in London to create the right cover before undertaking the assignment.

Joshua and Aron explained to Sir Arthur that Michael was not a neophyte. He had artistic and design ability, as he had had grown up in fashion retail. The major purpose of his coming to London was to learn the administrative side of the business and create a history of being with the company. They would establish his personal history to withstand any scrutiny on the part of the Egyptians. They wanted Sir Arthur to apply immediately for licenses to develop retail stores in Egypt, principally Cairo. They believed the Egyptian Department of Commerce would be more than open to a Fantastique retail chain in Egypt. It was a country of more than seventy million. Even though poverty was rampant, it had the demographics of a better or medium-grade retail. It was a feasible project with all the reasons to become a legitimate plan. How far was the charade to go? That depended on the rest of the plan.

Michael was sent off to London and assumed his new identity. He had been an A student in the brief time he had for training. There really wasn't a choice, as Hassan was moving quickly and Michael, in his new identity, was the hope to be the countering force to bring him down.

There was an article in the British fashion press, picked up by many of the newspapers, announcing that Daniel Amin had received a major promotion at Fantastique and was destined to be a key executive for special projects. The history was well put together, and there was a paper trail that was easily accessible and current. Sir Arthur was pleasantly surprised to work with Michael. He had been told that he was talented, but naturally there was doubt. That soon disappeared, for Michael was able to hold his own and then some with Sir Arthur. They had found rooms for him in Mayfair near the office, and Michael adjusted to his new surroundings.

His major task was to create a reputation as a key executive in the company. Michael spent time with the British Fashion Council as a liaison with Fantastique. He was a prominent figure at London Fashion Week, developing his own reputation and that of the company.

The necessary Egyptian licenses were not that difficult to acquire. Michael established himself quickly and invited the director of Egyptian commerce to London, expenses paid, to finalize the contractual agreements. They were impressed with his professionalism and command of Arabic. It was coming together.

Michael used all the assets of the company that were at his disposal, for they had built or renovated thousands of stores. He was armed with myriad store designs and floor plans.

While at dinner, Sir Arthur commented, "Daniel, maybe this project is actually going to work. I know what you are after, and I know a retail business is not the number one priority on your list, but it could happen."

"I wouldn't count on it, but stranger things have happened." Michael thought. Once a retailer, always a retailer!

"Sir Arthur, I want to thank you for allowing me to be part of your organization. I can say that I not only enjoyed being here but that I have learned a lot from you and your people. I will always remember your kind hospitality and friendship."

"Michael, it has been a pleasure having you here. If by chance you decide you want to come and live in London, the doors are always open. May God keep you safe, and may this venture be successful for all concerned."

They had all been working hard to build Michael's cover. Aron and Joshua wanted Michael to be known as a playboy. They felt he had to have some sort of an image that would make his entrance into Egyptian society not only easier but more desirable. It was crucial to the plan, so they thought.

There was one more hurdle that had to be addressed, and it was one Joshua and Aron wished to avoid. Unfortunately, it was impossible, for Michael needed a British passport. They did not want to issue him a fake set of documents. They now had to go to M-16 to secure their part in the operation. It would have been impossible to achieve except that London had its issues with Hassan. He was supplying Northern Ireland, India, and rebels with weapons, and they were being used to kill British troops. Bringing a third party into the operation was the problem, and they davened over it for two days. The problem had to be addressed. There was no choice. They realized the whole operation could fail if they could not bring the British into the loop.

Aron had a long relationship with Johnathan Calhoun, the director of M-16. They had served together years before as part of the British forces fighting Rommel. They understood one another, and Aron filled him in on the entire plan. The British and the Israelis had a mutual goal to keep the Suez Canal open. The possibility of Hassan supplying Nasser for the purpose of building rockets and new armed forces was not in the interests of the British in the region. The balance of power in the Middle East, as well as the State of Israel, was at risk. A deal was struck with Aron giving his word the British would be kept in the loop.

Michael, now Daniel Amin Hussein, was ready. He had been in London for two months and was getting "itchy" to take the next step. Fantastique, through their travel department, had scouted out living arrangements that would fit his situation and put him in the heart of the better residential area of Cairo. Aron and Joshua wanted to make sure Michael's residence would be in a perfect location for him to join "the beautiful people" of Cairo. It was an absolute necessity for this to work. Northeast of Cairo's center of historic districts was the wealthy residential suburb of Heliopolis. It was the home of Nasser and the political, industrial, and influential leaders of the country. Here Michael found his living quarters, which were already furnished. The only change Michael made was to opt for a king-size bed! It was a pleasant apartment, rather large, with more than sufficient light. He checked it over for possible devices. It was part of what he learned in his educational process. He hired a woman to clean and shop for his breakfast meals and keep the refrigerator stocked with snacks. Lunch and dinner most nights were at the local restaurants.

He wanted to get his bearings and scout the city for several reasons. His purpose there was to find a location for the retail operation and office. He needed to make a connection with an Egyptian who had been working for the Israelis for several years. This was to be done very cautiously and not until he was set up on the business side of his projects. How this would be done was not entirely worked out yet. They wanted the connection to happen; it was absolutely crucial.

The decision was finally made that contacting this person would only take place when there was an absolute necessity. As an employee of Fantastique, Michael had the option to return to London at any time under the pretext of meetings or related matters. He would be able to meet with Aron and Joshua and work out any issues or strategies there.

The Egyptian Retail Commercial Council wined and dined Michael. They wanted Fantastique to be the initial better retailer to open in Egypt and bring a whole international group of retailers to the country. The council invited a mixed group of additional guests to the dinners, ranging from various areas of the government to private industry.

CHAPTER ELEVEN

THE MAJOR PART OF THE PLAN NEEDED TO UNFOLD. IT WAS ingenious on the part of Aron, who came up with the idea of getting Michael involved with EgyptCo, the manufacturing and marketing arm of the Hassan organization. Egyptco had developed a bedsheet and inexpensive apparel business using the resources of the country, Cotton. The need for Fantastique to use a domestic apparel source in their stores—not only for the coming operations in Egypt but the opportunity to be a major customer for two thousand units—was a situation any resource would desire. It would put Michael, as the buyer, in position to spend time in the Hassan organization.

Hassan had word of Michael's coming and the plan for Fantastique to develop retail. He was extremely interested when he heard that Michael was considering buying his product for the entire chain. With stores around the globe, it gave him a vehicle to ship his "additional" products with greater ease. It seemed like a good opportunity to use EgyptCo to help his armament business. For that reason, he invited Michael to break bread. Hassan brought along Doria, his managing director, to see how this person could be of use to their EgyptCo organization and possibly of use in other areas.

Hassan wanted to know everything about this person who came out of nowhere. He immediately called London and had his people find out everything they could about Daniel Hussein Amin.

He wanted a complete dossier on his desk before they had their dinner date.

"We want to make certain that Mr. Amin is who he says he is. He could have access in some way to our facilities that are out of bounds. There is an opportunity for some interesting business but only on a basis that does not expose any of our special projects."

Michael started his "hunt" for a location. The center of Cairo's downtown district was the Maydan Tahrir area. It was a mass of people, shops, restaurants, hotels, and a wide variety of commercial establishments. Tahrir Square, translated into English as Liberation Square, was also known as Martyr Square. It was a gathering place for protests and demonstrations over the years. The area also included museums, gardens, and art galleries. Cairo's inhabitants flocked to the center, for it also had views of the Nile.

This was the logical place for a retail operation. You could not find a more desirable location, for the traffic was almost impossible to measure.

Michael, or should we say Daniel Amin, was adjusting to his new environment. The language was not an issue. He had been speaking Arabic to his mentors, Aron and Joshua, for weeks before leaving. He now had all the nuances and idiomatic expressions of any Egyptian, if needed. He found a small office in the Maydan Tahrir area. It was not necessary to hire any staff at the time, and he really didn't want any for privacy reasons. He would address that point when necessary as he negotiated a working arrangement with a real estate agency to help secure a location for the flagship unit. He found a contemporary furniture company and furnished the office in one afternoon.

Hassan's intelligence on Daniel Hussein Amin was all positive, and he seemed to be who he said he was. Fantastique was a major player in the world fashion market, and Hassan could not see any reason why he should not work with and trust Mr. Amin; well, trust to a certain extent! Even though that was the case, Hassan decided to have his people take a look at Michael's apartment just to dot all the i's and cross the t's. It was not bugged but was gone over with a fine-tooth comb. On top of that, he asked Nasser to use the General Intelligence Directorate to run a check on Fantastique and Mr. Amin. This was Egypt's equivalent to M15 and M-16 and the CIA. It was under the supervision of Salah Nasr, who happened to live in the same condominium complex as Michael. Michael was aware that someone had been in his condominium. Nothing was missing and everything was in its proper place, but somehow, it was not exactly how he had left it. Aron and Joshua had warned him to expect that he would be under suspicion and would more than likely be searched. He was prepared for it and readjusted his suits in the closet so he would know if it was ever done again.

Michael could not contain his excitement when he got the call from Hassan's administrative assistant to set up a dinner meeting. They were to meet at Maestro's, an Italian restaurant located in the Intercontinental Hotel in Heliopolis. Michael knew the hotel and the restaurant. Hassan was the true host, for he sent a chauffeured limousine to pick him up.

"Mr. Amin, or should I call you Daniel? Although I was brought up in Germany, I prefer the personal tense instead of waiting twenty years before we both agreed." Michael laughed and agreed immediately as they spoke in Arabic.

"Would you prefer English? I see that your Arabic is impeccable."

"I have spoken Arabic my whole life. In fact, it was my only language for the first five or six years of my life."

"I hope you don't mind but I have invited some other interesting guests. They should be arriving shortly."

As he spoke, Doria Sadat entered. Michael could not take his eyes off her as she made her way to the table accompanied by a gentleman, Salah Nasr.

"Let me introduce Mr. Hussein Amin to you all. We welcome him and his company to Egypt, hoping that his desire to build a business here will be successful."

Doria wore a black pantsuit with a white camisole that came across as the perfect outfit. She had simple, exquisite silver jewelry to accent the suit. It looked like it came from a small boutique he knew of in Paris. Her shoes were quite simple but unusual, as they had studded ornamentation. She was a knockout! Nasr, on the other hand, was not a fashion plate, as his suit was a few years old. His eyes never left Michael, and you could tell he was Secret Service.

To Michael's surprise, they ordered drinks. They were not Muslims who abstained from alcohol. In fact, they looked as if they were sitting in New York or London enjoying dinner. Hassan put down his martini and turned to Michael.

"So, Daniel, tell us about you. Who are you? We are curious to know about you and your company."

"Well, as you probably know, I grew up in the UK but spent formidable years in the United States going to Rhode Island School of Design and Brown University, ending up in the Harvard Business School. I have worked for Fantastique since I was fifteen years old during my schooling and summer vacations. I consider myself a seasoned employee. My English is now American rather than British, after spending over six years in the States. My employment with Fantastique has been unbelievable. Sir Arthur has given me the opportunity to grow and advance. We are dedicated as a company to grow our business worldwide and have taken on the opportunity to grow here in Egypt. I have only been here a short time, but I believe we are in the right place at the right time, looking for the right partners, which seem to be you."

Doria had not really entered the conversation until this time. "Daniel, where are you living, and how are you getting along in your social life? We want to make sure you are not sitting home reading romance novels. We heard you were part of the scene in London!" Everyone chuckled.

"Well, I could use some help. My reading material is extremely boring."

The topic turned to business, with Hassan leading the conversation.

"I know you have just started to look for possible locations through a real estate agency. Believe me, we want to help. I brought Mr. Nasr along so that if you need any government help, he would gladly use his influence with any of the landlords. Besides, I don't think you realize that he is your neighbor." Nasr smiled and nodded his head in agreement.

"I brought Doria along. As you more than likely know, she has been my right hand in managing all our communications and runs our subsidy, EgyptCo. We feel we can offer you great Egyptian cotton products made to your specifications, not only for your future stores here but to supply all of Fantastique. We want to be a major supplier and feel we have the product, quality-wise, as well as competitive pricing to be a key resource!"

Michael was very positive. "I should look at what your product line represents and visit your manufacturing facilities. There is no question that we could bring the technology and styling elements to make this happen. We have done it in Asia, principally Hong Kong and Thailand. Why not here in Egypt?"

Michael could see that he had scored points with Hassan and Doria. Nasr sat there with the same expression on his face as before.

Doria summed up her thoughts "I would like to take you to our manufacturing facilities and get your opinion on our programs. I realize we are not as experienced as other countries developing cotton apparel, but we have potential to be a competitor in the world market. Our labor pool is tremendous and can compete price-wise with any country."

It was working. He now had the possibility of access to their complex. EgyptCo facilities were part of a major group of buildings where Hassan stocked his weapon purchases. It was where he distributed the necessary materials for Nasser to build the V-2 rockets. All the research run by the German scientists was done within the walls of their facilities.

Michael suppressed his excitement over the conversation. As much as he wanted to get started as soon as possible, he told Doria that he was involved with the real estate project and would appreciate seeing the facilities in about a week to ten days.

Doria felt that she had sold Michael on seeing their operations and being open to the possibility of doing business together. "You need someone to be your tour guide in this great city and introduce you to the beautiful people. I will be your guide if you wish."

"How could I refuse an invitation offered from such a beautiful woman?" Doria laughed and they commenced with eating their dinner.

Hassan kept asking Michael question after question. Michael was well schooled and redirected the conversation into areas where Hassan was not experienced. Michael asked questions about Egypt, and the answers came from Doria, not Hassan. There was no question that Hassan and Doria were impressed with him.

Michael countered with a question: "Your basic business is making cotton bedsheets and low-end apparel. Do you feel you have the mentality to move in some fashion product?"

Hassan studied Michael. "I don't understand the question."

"Well, it isn't just setting up a manufacturing line to develop the material and product. It is an entirely different process. We are not making cookies, the same cookie every day. In this business, it takes flexibility and creativity to solve the problems that are sure to arise in this endeavor. A new development for the Third World is always suspect to failure, not because of product but the inability of management to make it work."

"I would hope that with your help, we will not fall into that trap. We are willing to give you full control of the process."

They seemed to like him and believed that he was who he said he was. Suspicion was built into their personalities. It was all business, and that meant covering every issue.

Nasr said nothing and voiced no opinion until they later talked among themselves. He was just there to observe and could not say anything positive or negative about the person or the evening.

Hassan thought for a moment and said, "So, our new friend and possible business associate, let's go forward with a program that Doria laid out. Come visit our facilities, and we can then talk intelligently as to how we should proceed."

Hassan lifted his glass and asked for a toast. "A new beginning" were his words as they clinked glasses. They had coffee and dessert. Michael passed on the dolce but had a double espresso.

He could see there was the possibility of chemistry between him and Doria. It was very subtle, but he felt there was something more than just wanting to make a business deal. Maybe he was wishing it would happen, for she had made a lasting impression, not just sexually but he liked everything about her actions. Was this going to be a problem? It was not the ideal situation and was something he had not counted on. His first thoughts were to dismiss the possibility that she was more than just another woman. He needed to focus on the plan.

As he got out of the limo, he believed the evening had been very successful. The plan was working, and he seemed to have initially sold himself to his antagonists. They were very clever, and he thought he might have been taped by Mr. Nasr. He just had that feeling.

"Thank you for a great evening. I am looking forward to seeing the plant and discussing the possibilities that arise."

There was a new development in the plan, and he initiated it. The way into the organization was through their desire to be a resource for Fantastique. He had considered this strategy along with the retail situation. What made things clearer was the possibility that he had found an opening. It became very evident this road brought him closer to achieving the goal.

As he entered his apartment, total exhaustion came over him. He had been on a high with the adrenaline driving him to be at his best for this meeting. He felt a sense of accomplishment and, at the same time, realized this was not child's play. He was about to be playing with fire and people's lives.

Michael opened the refrigerator, took out the Pellegrino, and poured himself a half glass. He walked into the bedroom and saw the message light was on. It was Doria with a short message: "Enjoyed the conversation and looking forward to showing you the city and our facilities."

He was flattered that she left the message, but at the same time, a bell was ringing somewhere in his psyche. He remembered a saying from Robert Frost: "Don't ever take a fence down until you know why it was put up."

Sleep was his priority as he slipped off his clothes, and before he knew it, he was dreaming of Doria, floating down the Nile together. They were as close as one could be, just about to kiss, when a python appeared around their waists. Michael awoke sweating. In the morning, as he turned on the shower, the gushing cold stream emphasized the situation. He was in it up to his neck, maybe more.

Cairo was a teeming, steaming metropolis, with people everywhere. In a way, it worked for him. You could melt into the crowd and become anonymous. It would take a series of professional stalkers to find him in the heart of the city. He meandered around trying to get his bearings. Michael wanted to know the city as a native, for he thought there would be a time when it would be needed.

To the east of the center was the walled medieval section of the city known as Islamic Cairo, which included the poor residential districts. There you could find historic architecture dating back more than a thousand years and the bustling Khan al-Khalili marketplace. Its main street, Sharia al Mu'izz, was lined with structures from several eras of Egyptian history including those before the Ottoman era. Garden City, south of Maydan Tahrir, was the upscale district with

I Shall Know Who I Am

expensive homes and numerous embassies. He wanted to know, if needed, how to reach the British or US embassies.

To the east was an area dominated by the Citadel, a medieval fortress that was home to Egypt's rulers for some seven hundred years, as well as many mosques and museums. There was the exclusive suburb of Zamalek, Cairo's wealthiest neighborhood, occupying two-thirds of the island of Gezirah. The rest was private sport clubs and parks. He made himself aware of all these "neighborhoods" and gained a working knowledge of the city. A necessary meeting with an Egyptian contact was imminent, and he wanted to pick the meeting place. The only way he could contact Aron and Joshua without flying to London was through this contact or by sending a coded telex to Sir Arthur at Fantastique. He had not yet reached a situation where he felt it was necessary.

He had his marching orders to infiltrate, in one manner or another, the Hassan organization and to identify the locations and actual facilities where the weapons were located. Other areas were high on the Israelis' list, such as the need to identify as many key German scientists and former military personnel who were working for Nasser and also associated with Hassan. He felt by joining the social circle of Hassan and possibly Nasser himself he could gain the necessary information.

The personal part of his decision to work with Israel was to find out if his cousins were still alive and in Cairo or Egypt. Aron and Joshua had promised Michael, one way or another, that if they were alive they would find a way to bring them to Israel. Their promise was predicated on Michael being focused on the plan to destroy Hassan and the program Nasser had developed with the German scientists. Michael had given Aron and Joshua his word that he would live by the bargain. It was difficult not to try to find them on his own, but he would live by his word. He believed Aron and Joshua would make good on their promises.

Michael was counting the days before he called Doria and asked her to show him the EgyptCo facilities and product. He waited just more than a week before he contacted her. The delay served the purpose of showing that Fantastique was not "pushing" for a relationship. It was just the opposite. Michael was betting the whole operation on making a deal that would bring him into their organization.

Doria came on the line. "Daniel, so glad to hear from you. I was concerned that you forgot about us. I hope things are going well and you're still enthused about seeing our facilities."

"No, I was tied up with the real estate agency and handling telexes, which are still my responsibility in the goings-on in London. So let's make a time to get together."

"The sooner the better, as far as I am concerned. I would like to coordinate your visit with spending some time with Hassan. He is free tomorrow and I am as well, so let me pick you up at 9:00 a.m. and we will spend the day. I can guarantee it will be interesting!"

What struck Michael was that she was speaking English and not Arabic. Naturally, he answered in the same. Her English was without an accent and showed a tinge of her being a Londoner. He then remembered that some of her education had taken place in London.

Michael asked himself a question: "How Westernized has she become?"

CHAPTER TWELVE

EGYPT FROM THE 1952 REVOLUTION ON WAS FURTHER advanced industrially than other Arab countries in Africa or the Middle East, except South Africa. Under the Nasser government, they pressed for industrial expansion and the establishment of an industrial base. Greater Cairo, Alexandria, and Heiwan were the main Egyptian industrial areas. They produced iron, steel, textiles, and petro chemicals. The clothing and textile sectors were the largest industrial employers.

Hassan had all his operations in Heiwan. It is a city south of Cairo considered part of greater Cairo on the banks of the Nile opposite the ruins of Memphis. His extensive operations were located here in a massive industrial zone completely encompassed with the latest security, communications, and electrified fencing. He had his own security force. The facility not only housed Hassan's holdings, but Nasser had joined his operations with him to build weapons using German technicians and scientists. Hassan was not enamored with the arrangement, for he had to answer in part to government bureaucracy, and that was always a problem.

As Michael entered the limousine, Doria gave him a smile and a two-handed clasp of his hand.

"So we are off to see our operations. We are heading south of the city, hopefully quickly. The traffic can be brutal."

Michael reached into his briefcase. "I brought along photos of the latest fashion goods we've purchased and how they will be displayed in our operations. We could go over them now. It will give you a general idea of what our tastes are and where your strengths fit into an opportunity to work and produce in these areas."

They leafed through the photos. Doria would comment on any articles that seemed to fit their strengths. She had a good taste level and seemed to have a better than average sense of fashion and merchandising.

"I really like what you're making for the stores. I hope we can do something similar."

"So what did you think of my boss? I can tell you right now you got high marks from him. Hassan does not usually express himself so positively about anyone."

Michael smiled. "I'm flattered, but I really would like to know what Mr. Nasr, my neighbor and Secret Service person, thinks about me."

They both laughed. There were many questions back and forth, and both seemed to enjoy the repartee. Again, it was all in English, which didn't bother Michael but made him slightly suspicious. The dinner meeting was conducted in Arabic. Why English now? Was it aimed at trying to discover something, or did she like the practice?

They finally arrived, and he suggested in future visits they should get an early start to avoid the traffic. The facilities were huge and the security was even more restrictive than he thought. Everyone, including Doria, went through a screening system as if they were to board an airplane. They went directly to Doria's office, which was located in a building connected to the showrooms, product area, and manufacturing area.

"So what do you want to see first?"

"As you know, Doria, I am a product person interested in design and the manufacturing process, so let's start there."

They started walking through the production facility. It was well organized and seemed to run efficiently. The production lines for both the development of the fabric and the actual manufacture of the bedsheets were in full gear.

"We are self-sufficient in every phase of production. Let me tell you about Egyptian cotton. The main difference is that regular cotton and Egyptian cotton come from different plants, so their properties are never going to be the same. Our cotton is handpicked, which puts less stress on the fibers, leaving them straight and intact. These fibers can be made longer to create very fine yarns without sacrificing length. It creates a stronger, softer product unlike regular cotton. Since our pure cotton consists of finer thread, it can be woven into each square inch and produce a finer, more consistent finish ending up as a softer and more flexible fabric. As it has not been picked by machines, the fibers are stronger and more resistant to stress. Our product guarantees the highest level of purity and has the ability to absorb liquids, meaning deeper and more resistant colored fabrics. It translates to vivid colorations. We have been specializing in bed linens and have developed a significant worldwide business. We feel we can become a major player with our cotton for fashion shirts and other apparel. With your help to develop the product, Fantastique can have a wonderful collection at 25 percent below the market. Well, that's my sales pitch. Let me show you how it happens."

Michael was impressed. He did not expect to hear such a presentation and was amazed with the production process. He spent the better part of the morning seeing how the material was developed into actual product.

"I have to say, you have shown me some methods of producing interesting fabrications. I see great potential for us."

Michael was contemplating how he should proceed. He realized that if he spent time here, he could eventually, with some luck, pinpoint the operations that were being developed for Nasser. He needed to know exactly where Hassan's materials and chemicals were housed. He had to work out a plan that would allow him to survey the whole complex. The question was: how could he sell it to Hassan so he would give him more access to the facility?

Hassan was keenly interested in Michael's comments during lunch. He praised Doria for her expertise and her overall running of the operation. Michael had that uncanny ability to analyze the problem and come up with a solution. In this instance, it was skill in product development, along with the skill to solve problems.

"You both know you have a major opportunity to become a real player in the apparel field. You have all the building blocks: material, cheap labor, and self-financing. What are you missing? Someone like our company and myself who can make it happen. The problem is that it cannot be done without a major commitment on both parts. You need my help to put the pieces together. I am proposing the following: I will put together a team of seasoned technicians who can work with me to achieve our goals. We will set up a new production line exclusively for us that will commence with making fashion shirts for women. I am intrigued by your fabrications. We will start with a short line, basically to produce sample production. We should move forward on this basis.

"I will need to stay here three to four full days a week. It will demand some type of adequate sleeping quarters. I can eat with the workers. It is not an issue. You are working two shifts now, so it will not be a problem. How long will it take? That's difficult to say, but if there is total, and I mean total, cooperation, we will see major results in six to eight months. All of this came to me when I walked through the factory. I saw it as doable when I heard Doria's knowledge of the product and your desire to develop this segment of your business!

"Let's be super honest. Fantastique will benefit greatly from this project. A 25 to 30 percent advantage in cotton apparel will give us a monopolistic position in the market. I feel if we do this right, it will even create a greater advantage. I would need to go to London and work this out with Sir Arthur and our staff. This project must be done right or it will not work. Total effort is needed to meet our goals. A joint venture done right that fulfills all the points I brought up should bring a great return for us both. What do you think?"

Hassan sat there. He had a cigarette in his hand and he stubbed it out in his salad plate and turned to look at Doria, who had not said a word. "Daniel, you are some salesman. I've heard 'pitches' before but none quite so passionate and, at the same time, making sense for both parties. Can you put a number on the project?"

"It will cost, but in the overall scheme of things, will be inexpensive. That's my only political statement." They all laughed.

Michael sipped his coffee. "I will have to go to London shortly and talk to our technical staff and put together a real plan. I know Sir Arthur; he built his business on positioning product development as the primary source for success. I need to work out the details."

On the return trip to his apartment, Doria was not that talkative. She was pleased the way Michael handled Hassan. She knew he was not an "easy mark," and gaining his confidence and having him sign off on this project caught her off guard. She looked at Michael in a different light. He would now be a partner in developing this program and, at the same time, a person with his own agenda, different from theirs. She was ecstatic over his comments and, at the same time, guarded.

There was another element entering the scene. She was being drawn toward Michael. He was everything she admired: creative, intelligent, sensual. Doria felt that he was difficult to read. What were his intentions? Was he interested in a personal relationship? Was it wise to allow herself to be vulnerable? All these questions seemed to resonate as they made the drive.

Michael sat back and closed his eyes. He felt he was climbing Everest and now had the path to the summit. Doria was a beautiful woman, and being drawn to her seemed problematic. She was a very different person than he had ever experienced. There definitely was magnetism between the two. They were drawn to one another, and their feelings would be difficult to control. Her physical beauty made it impossible to keep his eyes off her. He was impressed with her ability to articulate her thoughts whether they were personal or business-related.

The problem was that she was the enemy. Do you want to be literally in a bed with your nemesis? He dozed for a few minutes. His dream consisted of having her in his arms. When they arrived at Michael's, there were pleasantries between them. Doria gave him an opening when she suggested introducing him to Cairo's society.

"What I said the other night, I meant. I don't want you sitting at home watching TV or reading yesterday's *Herald Tribune*."

"I prefer to be with you rather than reading the editorials."

Michael had to make arrangements to return to London. He needed to sit down with Aron and Joshua and work out a strategy that he initiated. Michael had come up with this plan, pulling it out of the air at the spur of the moment. It was an "idea" that was never on the table with Tel Aviv. It was a plan that was not worked out in advance, but the original plan was to find a way into Hassan's complex. He was in desperate need of their advice, expertise, and inventiveness. The other issue was now involving Sir Arthur in a venture that was not part of the original plan. Would he do it?

He now had to decide how he wanted to proceed with the Michael plan. Aron and Joshua would want to know the details on how he envisioned the strategy. It would be difficult to sell them . . . period. The more he tossed the idea around, the more he believed it could work.

His thoughts turned toward Doria. Was he taking his eyes off the ball, letting his feelings rise to the surface? It was a trying situation, for the heart brought out all his emotions and could unduly influence his judgment. His temporary decision was, "Let's see how it plays out". An evening out with Doria and friends was far better than the reading material on hand.

Michael began making plans to return to London. He contacted the guys by sending a telex to the travel agency that was really an agency of the Mossad company. They would respond with an itinerary for his departure.

Joshua and Aron, upon receiving the information, were concerned. They expected Michael to come back to London but not so soon. Something was not right, and it sent up flags for their program and Michael's safety. Was he up to the task? Was he having second thoughts? They were in the dark, and that was, in their estimation, the worst possible scenario. They gave him a date to meet.

Michael was slightly nervous, and he kept looking at his watch, wanting time to move faster for his "date" with this beautiful and interesting woman. Maybe the excitement of living close to the edge was what he enjoyed. He was very angry with himself, for he realized this was not a good sign. His emotions were overwhelming his good sense.

They had dinner and the conversation came around to Doria and her history, which Michael already knew from her dossier. She was very forthcoming and gave him a story that fit the information he had acquired through the Israelis. What he did learn was that here was a woman who had all the assets he desired in a possible partner. Michael was very attentive, looking for any areas that were questionable. He gave her a quick rundown on who he was and a résumé of his business life. There was no question she had read a report on him from the security agencies of Egypt.

Michael was positive. "I am fairly certain Sir Arthur will bless the proposition I put to you and Hassan. It is a way for all of us to achieve a new venue of profits. If that's the case, you will need to do your part, starting with finding a place for me to stay in the factory for three to four nights. This is key, Doria. I will need your total cooperation to get the operation going. We will need to lay out a plan for the sample production line."

"I will get on it this week. It will be quite easy to get this done. We have facilities for some of our engineers and technical people who are working on other projects for the Egyptian government, so the living facilities are there."

Michael was ecstatic and had to control his excitement. He had found a way in. Now came selling it to London and Tel Aviv.

They had a fairly early dinner for Egypt dining. The plan for the evening was to meet Doria's friends and the expats. Hopefully some of the Germans involved in Hassan's programs. Doria took him to a private club frequented by the well-to-do Egyptians and expats. She had an ulterior motive, watching him mingle. Was he a flirt with anything that had a skirt? How did he handle himself?

Michael was focused on finding ex-Nazis involved in the projects. He searched the room to see if he could identify any. During his "education," he was shown some photos of known Nazis they believed were in Egypt working on the projects. He thought he recognized two of them. They were playing billiards and speaking German. He wanted to know if Doria knew them, for then she could possibly introduce him. Michael sat on a stool and watched them play. As he drank his beer, Doria wandered back to where he was sitting.

"Daniel, I want you to meet some of your possible roommates, Karl Steiger and Alex Hirsch. They are involved in our operations, or should I say President Nasser's projects."

They shook hands and passed a few words before they continued with the game Michael confirmed recognized them from his photo sessions. He filed their names and photos away and would discuss them with Joshua and Aron. Doria's friends appeared. They were all sophisticated, well-dressed, business-oriented men and women who asked question after question about London, Fantastique, and Michael's life story. Doria sat there taking it in. Every once in a while, Michael gave her a look that read "Get me out of here." She finally rescued him from the "inquisition," and they left. Doria took him to a small café around the corner. They sat there staring at one another for what seemed like an eternity until the waiter arrived.

Michael felt he was in trouble, for his feelings for Doria were very real. His defense mechanisms were not responding, and his heart was in a contest with his mission. They ordered coffee. Egyptian coffee was brewed by using hot sand and had a heater under it. It involved taking very finely ground coffee from a Turkish coffee grinder and then heating it to a boil repeatedly in a container know as an Ibrik.

Doria was feeling the pressure of how she should handle this unforeseen problem of being drawn toward Michael. She had only known him a short time, and just superficially, but she knew she was being drawn to him and could not resist. She was losing control, and that was not an option. It had never happened to her before, and she was completely caught off guard.

"I really enjoyed your friends, even though they grilled me as if I was under arrest!"

Doria smiled. "I saw that you were struggling with the barrage of questions. I should have rescued you sooner."

They laughed. There was small talk, with Michael taking the lead, telling her about his experiences in the US and the like. She wanted to know everything about the States, and Michael could sense it was her desire to find a way there.

"I've had this love affair with America. My father used to tell me stories about New York and his work in Chicago. He was a visiting professor at Columbia and the University of Chicago. He wanted to migrate there, but it never materialized."

She spoke of Hassan always with gratitude for giving her the opportunity to be a key person in his organization and for recognizing her ability. They sat there for two hours telling each other not only about their lives but their dreams.

After three coffees and endless conversation that stripped away any facades, they were joking with one another and flirting, along with a display of body language. They were headed toward problems once they threw caution to the wind.

Michael then took her by the hand and gave her a hug. "It has been a wonderful evening, and I cannot begin to thank you for being such a generous hostess. I feel we are going to be great friends, apart from our business relationship. I know you are anxious, as am I, to see our business and personal relationships grow. We are both wanting to go at breakneck speed to make it happen. It's been a great evening, but it's time for the sandman. Let's sleep on all those ideas we have talked about. So I am putting you in your limo and taking a taxi home."

She smiled and gave him a sisterly hug. Michael thought the situation was defused for the time being, but it was only the first inning of what he believed would be an extra-innings game.

The "travel agency" came back with his itinerary, Cairo to London on BOAC Airways. The flight was booked for Wednesday, which was the day after tomorrow. They wanted to see him as quickly as possible. Michael spent the following day looking at the real estate issues. He went through the motions, knowing it was not the answer to their problems. The charade had to be played. His idea of developing Hassan's facility, EgyptCo, was the way to the objective. He spoke with Doria, giving her his itinerary, and asked her to arrange all the details for his return.

"I will be gone probably a week and will give you and Hassan a call as soon as I get clearance for the plan. In the meantime, I want you to go ahead with setting me up at your facility. If you are home this evening, I will give you a call."

"Call me after 9 p.m. and we can speak. I will go ahead as if the program has been approved. We both seem to be very positive about our future together."

Michael hung up the phone with a smile on his face. What did "future together" mean? Was it just the business side, or did it mean more? He was thinking about her words all day. Michael was well aware he had to be careful. Phones can be tapped and recorded. He had the impression Hassan would not be pleased if there was a romantic interlude or more with her. He was on dangerous ground and realized a romance had to be avoided. His thoughts were interrupted. The phone rang, and it was Hassan. "I wanted to reach you before you left for London. I have spoken with Doria and have a good feeling, as does she, that we are embarking on a great project. I assure you we will do our part to make it successful."

They talked about how he was getting along and what he could do to help the social scene. "I don't think you will have any problems with Doria directing you."

"It certainly seems that way. Her friends could not have been nicer, with all kinds of invitations."

"Bon voyage! Call me from London if you need anything."

Later that evening he spoke with Doria. The conversation covered Hassan's call and was very business-oriented. He asked her many questions about the ability to get pattern makers and experienced sample-room people. Michael wanted to be able to interview these key people on his return.

"What would you like me to bring you from London, as long as it fits in my suitcase?"

"You remember I went to school in London and developed a taste for smoked salmon. You could get it at Harrod's just before returning. I will make some hors d'oeuvres for us. Have a safe trip!"

CHAPTER THIRTEEN

THE FLIGHT WAS IN THE MORNING AND WAS UNEVENTFUL. First-class service was quite good, and Michael arrived refreshed around early evening London time. He didn't have anyone meet him and went directly to his apartment, wanting to reach the guys as soon as possible. He expected a message of some sort on his machine. He was tired but not ready to rest. After showering and a change of clothes, he thought of going out, possibly to the office. Someone had stocked the refrigerator. He thought it was the cleaning lady, but then he realized it was one of Aron's people here in London. They were looking after him The phone message was straight to the point "There is a product-development meeting at the office at nine o'clock. Rest well. See you tomorrow." He had second thoughts about going out. Instead he sat down at his desk and started to put his ideas in order. It wasn't the best time to work, but his mind was running a hundred miles a minute. He awoke about three hours later in his swivel chair, papers on the floor and in a daze. Night was upon him, and as he disrobed, his thoughts were of the next day and Doria.

Aron and Joshua were waiting for him as he exited the apartment. They had arrived two days before and met with Sir Arthur to set up the meeting today. They followed his taxi looking for any surveillance. Sir Arthur's major issue was to make sure Michael was safe. He did not care about whatever else happened so long as he was well.

They went to the Fantastique office and had a private conference room in the director's office available to them. Sir Arthur was asked to let them work with Michael before he joined the meeting. Michael gave them a blow-by-blow account of his weeks in Egypt. He had made notes on the plane and additional ones at his desk. He took them through every step of his journey. The plan, in his estimation, was the only way they could achieve maximum results. Naturally, it depended on Sir Arthur's willingness to go along with Fantastique being more involved than originally discussed.

Michael summed up his presentation after two hours of constant oratory.

"Number one, we can get to the heart of the situation much easier and quicker if we take this product-development route rather than a hit-or-miss position, faking a retail setting.

Number two, the ability to identify the Nazi staff working for Nasser is attainable by putting this plan into action.

Number three, we would be playing to our strength, for Hassan was not experienced in this business. Therefore, dependence on me and Fantastique would give us a much better chance of succeeding.

Number four, is there greater risk? Possibly, but definitely greater gain."

There was a lot to go over, but now they brought Sir Arthur into the meeting. Michael presented most of the story that they agreed to share with him. Aron and Joshua did the rest.

Sir Arthur looked at the three of them. "You are definitely out of your fucking minds, and now you want me to join the club. I will do anything for Israel, but when it gets into the realm of insanity, what do you expect me to do? You are all meshuganas! Yes, you have my help in any way!"

There was work to do, as the plan was complicated and dangerous, and demanded perfect execution. They decided all their work was to be done at Fantastique's offices. If anyone were watching Michael's movements, they would see him going to the office every day. They were not far from wrong. Hassan hired a surveillance company to check if Michael's credentials were real and if he was working daily at Fantastique.

Aron and Joshua anticipated and recognized the surveillance and played it to their advantage. It reinforced Michael's position with Hassan.

The sessions continued. They devised a new approach, for the Israelis had some interesting ideas that could give Michael options on achieving the destruction of the facilities. They arranged to give him additional help to develop the product line for Hassan. There was a need for production and quality-control staff. It was Aron's job to find people in Israel who could fill these positions. He had the perfect cover. Fantastique was sending the technicians to ensure the operation was successful. The investment on the part of the company was significant. The major need was the technical end—specifically pattern making. The patterns would be made in Fantastique's product-development center to ensure the samples and any production trials would be made properly. Hopefully, Michael would be able to use all the facilities of Fantastique to cut through a long-drawn-out development cycle.

It took long days to organize all the components, and the week just evaporated. They had managed to piece it all together and it seemed workable, if it all clicked. That was the big "if," and they all knew they needed to perform without a hiccup to ensure getting the job done and reaching safety.

Two days before finishing, Michael placed a call to Hassan and gave him a rundown of what they worked out. He congratulated Michael, not only on selling the association to Sir Arthur but on achieving a detailed course of action.

"I cannot believe you were able to accomplish that agenda in a week. We are fortunate to have you and will do everything in our power to work with you and your team. Doria happens to be in my office. Please speak with her."

"Daniel, my best wishes! You pulled it off. We were concerned that your company would not go along with your ideas."

"Thanks. I will be back in a few days. There will be a need for two additional rooms for my people who will control certain aspects of the development and production process. Let's get together shortly after I arrive."

"I will do one better. I will meet the flight. Just telex me the details." She hung up the phone.

Hassan looked at her. "My dear, let's be careful with Mr. Amin. All looks extremely positive. Sometimes that scares me. I am not a lover of the British, even though he is of Arabic descent."

The trio had a final meeting. They went over the checklist they had created and retraced the steps needed to reach their goal. The guys warned Michael not to underestimate Hassan, for he showed he was still suspicious.

During his stay in Israel and London, Michael had been in contact with Hannah at least once or twice a week. He tried to keep up with what was happening with his mother and sister. When he was about to start "traveling," he told Hannah that it would be difficult to communicate on a regular basis for a few weeks, possibly a month.

She did not ask questions. Hannah had complete faith in his actions. "Michael, reach me when you can. Stay safe!"

He felt uneasy. He had a wonderful relationship with his mother and sister. Michael was upset he could not tell her what had occurred and where he was going. In all his years, there was never a time where he obscured the truth from her. When he hung up the phone, he was upset with himself.

He called Abe and Sarah, telling them all about his travels in Israel. London was not mentioned.

During the London meetings, Michael again brought up his relatives. It was part of the bargain to find them and bring them to Israel.

Aron was direct and to the point. "One task at a time. We will not let you down. It is our work to bring every Jew home."

There was a sense of urgency. Real problems for Egyptian Jewry started in October 1956. Following the invasion of Britain, France, and Israel in the Suez Crisis, President Nasser brought in a set of sweeping legislations abolishing civil liberties, allowing the state to stage mass arrests without charges and to strip away Egyptian citizenship.

As part of the new policy, many professional positions were terminated. Many Jews were arrested and businesses were seized by the government. The actions were taken to encourage or expel foreign minorities—not only Jews but most Europeans. The decree included Egyptian Jews who were professionals or were suspected of having connections or relatives in Israel.

Those expelled were only allowed to take one suitcase and a small amount of cash. They were forced to sign declarations "donating" their property to the Egyptian government. There were incidents where Jewish families were taken hostage to ensure that no one spoke out against the government. Although many left, a significant number of Jews still remained in Egypt. Where were his relatives? Were they alive? Had they left? Could they leave? Michael wanted the answers. He believed Aron and Joshua would find a way.

CHAPTER FOURTEEN

WHEN HE DISEMBARKED, MICHAEL WAS MET BY A BOAC representative who sped him through immigration. The hand of Hassan was evident. Doria was there as he exited customs. Even though Michael was tired from the flight, he woke up looking at this spectacular woman who was smiling and centering her attention on him. He got a hug and a bouquet of flowers. Michael was slightly embarrassed over the show of affection. The limo was waiting, and they were off to his apartment. Doria insisted on helping him with his luggage and getting him settled.

"You look like you need sleep, lots of it. I guess the week was a nonstop work session. I was impressed that you could accomplish all your programs. Let me give you a couple days to recover, and we can then pick up all the points that need to be addressed."

"Thank you for meeting me, and for the flowers. All these gestures will get you anywhere you wish!"

She laughed. "Call me when you wish."

Michael fell into a deep sleep and vivid dreams followed. His Egyptian cousins were asking for his help. Doria was there tempting him to be more than a business partner. Aron and Joshua were giving him advice, and Hassan was having his people spy on him. It was a jumble of thoughts and filled his rest with turmoil. He awoke again with his mind in fourth gear.

Michael wanted to get the show on the road as quickly as possible. His priority was to relocate to Hassan's facility so he could put his plan into action. He needed to organize the product-development process. The pieces coming from Fantastique were in the works and, hopefully, would be here as soon as possible. They would be couriered here in less than two weeks, maybe sooner.

The two additional Israelis, who were supposedly production and quality-control technicians, needed to be put into action. He wanted Doria to find him some pattern makers and good sample-room people who could develop corrections and put the prototypes together. This was no easy task but was a necessity to get things moving. The operation had to be real. All of this was on his mind as he picked up the phone.

"Doria, good morning. I am feeling pretty good. The jetlag is not a factor, at least not now. We both are anxious to get things going, and I need to find out where you are on the points I asked you to handle."

They went over the agenda, and Doria gave him a rundown. "The accommodations for you and your techs will be ready in a few days. It is not a problem. Finding pattern people is another issue. They do not seem to exist. I would like to line up a few applicants and have you judge their ability. I do not believe that sample-room people, such as stitchers, are an issue if we are looking in the right places. When do you want to meet?"

"I need a day with my real estate people. I will call you tonight. I'll know a lot more by then."

When they spoke that evening, it was more personal than business. Doria wanted to know how all this work had affected him.

Michael was philosophical. "I guess I'm okay. There is no question that these last weeks have been hectic. When you are totally focused on developing the agenda, it takes its toll. I feel I have been fortunate to have found great partners in you and Hassan, mainly you, so I'm happy we have progressed at this sort of record-setting pace." He wanted to say more, but he hesitated, afraid he was being recorded. Michael could sense that Doria wanted to do the same but did not, probably for the same reason.

She picked him up the next morning. "You know, I won't have to do this in a few days. You will be living in the complex. Actually, I have a small apartment adjacent to my office that I use when necessary. If you need me for longer work sessions, I can easily conform to your schedule."

Michael didn't know how to interpret this. What was important was she would be available. Where it led was the obvious question. Michael reached into a bag and pulled out two pounds of smoked salmon and plunked it in her lap. "I didn't forget!" They laughed.

Michael came up with an idea that seemed to have merit. "Let's go to a fashion design school and see if there are students or instructors there that we can work with."

"Great idea. The Italian Fashion Academy in Cairo would be the place to consider."

They were pleasantly surprised to find several applicants who would be able to fill the position, for pattern-making was part of the curriculum. What they found were fit models who were perfect to show how the product appeared on real women who were considered model sizes. This would allow them to be okayed and graded for production. It solved a number of problems. The work would be done at the academy, for Michael wanted it this way. It was a good excuse to leave the complex if necessary. The pieces of the puzzle were coming together, or at least progressing at a pace that matched Michael's expectations. He was ready to tackle the reason why he was here.

The best-laid plans do not always work. Michael received a telex that his product people were delayed because of previous commitments and would be a week late. The patterns from Fantastique were being redone. Someone screwed them up. The wheels turn slowly in a corporation the size of Fantastique, even with priorities of the highest level.

Michael was being moved into his "new home." The apartment was a two-room suite that had all the necessary facilities: bedroom, kitchenette, a small studio type of setup. It had a television, cassette player, and most of the comforts of home. Doria had made sure everything was in order. Michael wanted his room to be located in the midst of the ex-Nazis. He couldn't request it, and what Doria designated was all that he could expect. When the work was finished, Doria took him for a visit and tour. There were a significant number of suites that seemed to be exactly like his. He presumed they were for the scientists working on Nasser's program.

"There is a main dining room if you wish." Doria had made arrangements for Michael's refrigerator to be stocked every day with salads, a main course that could be heated, and drinks and snacks.

Michael was now where he wanted to be. It could not have worked out better. The only hiccup was the two late technicians. The problem now was to get his missing comrades to Cairo. He kept his apartment, for he had the excuse of needing it to spend weekends there and when he worked with the Fashion Academy on patterns or fittings. The delay was frustrating and caused the timetable to be pushed back.

They went out to dinner after viewing the new residence.

"Michael, you have three or four days where you are waiting for critical parts of the project. I can see, as we say, 'you have ants in your pants.' I have an idea that will solve this problem."

"Please tell me."

Doria hesitated and then spoke. "You have seen none of this fantastic country. Let me take you on a trip to see what made Egypt the wonder of the ancient world and its heritage."

"Where will you take me? Do you have a note from your mother?"

"I will show you this country, not as a tour bus or museum guide but as a person who loves Egypt and is proud of its past and, yes, its present!"

"Well, what are we waiting for? I will pack a bag, and let's get started."

Michael didn't know what to expect or really where this was going. He had jumped at the chance, and it seemed to him that fate had brought this about. The gods had willed this. Could this be a positive situation? The jury was out, or, should I say, deliberating.

With all the discussions that went on in London with the Israelis, there was not one word about Doria. Either they had no inclination that Michael had any feelings for her or they did not say. Michael felt they knew everything he said or thought. He was excited about the whole impending holiday.

At the same time, he was concerned about how Tel Aviv would interpret this "deviation" from the plan. It would not be a positive situation in their eyes.

CHAPTER FIFTEEN

THEY STARTED THEIR TOUR IN CAIRO AT THE MUSEUM OF Egyptian Antiquities in Tahrir Square. She showed him the extensive collection of papyrus and coins dating back to the ancient world. They were in many languages and in many precious metals. There were artifacts from the New Kingdom, the time period between 1550 and 1069 BC. They included statues, sarcophagi, furniture in all sizes—artifacts from the final two dynasties of Egypt, including items of the Pharaohs as well as artifacts from the Valley of the Kings that were from the tombs of Tutankhamun and other pharaohs. She didn't want to get too specific but wanted Michael to catch the flavor of Egypt's majestic past. Michael thought of his mother and her involvement with the museum and the Egyptian collection.

In the garden, there was a memorial to the famous Egyptologists of the world who had brought this all to fruition. The statues and figurines were not only remarkable; they were exquisite. Michael's appreciation for art and his artistic sense made the tour there a rare experience.

They spent a good portion of the day here. Later, sitting in the garden, Doria gave him an additional history lesson as he tried to put everything he saw into perspective. The day just disappeared, and they stopped at a café in the square for a drink.

"Well, this was stop number one. We don't have time to see everything, but I thought one museum would suffice and give you a good idea of the past."

"I could not have been more pleased with your choice. It's hard to believe what transpired, putting it into today's world. But then again, you just can't really place yourself back in a world before Christ."

Doria pondered the statement for a moment. "I never asked you what, if any, religious denomination you're affiliated with. I presume you are a Muslim."

"So you could say that I am spiritual at this stage of my life. My parents are Muslim but not really practicing." Michael had to lie. He had no other choice. "And you? I would classify you as more or less spiritual. You do not come across in any way as the average Egyptian Muslim woman!" They laughed.

"No, that is certain. My parents never made religion the center point of their lives. Our whole social scene was in the academic world. I am in your camp. My two years in the UK were the deciding factors, shaping my whole life."

They sat there for quite some time people-watching. It seemed the world walked by Tahrir Square. It was a magnificent day, and the beauty of the moment was felt by both.

Doria took him to her favorite restaurant, El Fara. It was classic Egyptian cuisine. She was more or less a vegetarian, and the great mixture of vegetables, mashed fava beans, and Kushari—a mixture of lentils, rice, and pasta—were her choices. Michael just went along with her selections. He was not a vegetarian but just didn't feel like meat or a big meal. They drank wine, an "unknown" French brand, that probably was made in Egypt. It wasn't great but seemed to help the meal.

Doria put down her fork. "So what did you think of today? Would you give it high marks?"

"Probably so, but it's not over yet. You never know what could happen."

She smiled. "I guess that's very true. The world changes at a moment's notice. I've seen it happen. We are all unpredictable at times."

Michael was slightly uneasy and somewhat confused. Or should I say "he was neither on foot nor on horseback"? The question was how he should proceed with this woman he wanted to take to bed. They lingered over the meal and then coffee. The conversation covered a vast array of topics. It was less about the business and more about their lives.

Doria was very forthcoming with stories about her childhood and growing up in Alexandria. "My dad died a few years ago, and I decided to spend some time with my mother. They had a very close relationship, and it was difficult for her to be alone. I tried to get her to move to Cairo, but she wouldn't. I was very appreciative of my parents. They encouraged me to further my studies in London. It was a great experience that gave me a whole new perspective on my life. Living with a whole different concept of freedom was so new to me. This type of existence does not happen in Egypt. I almost decided not to return."

Michael reflected on her words. "I understand what you went through, for I can relate to your experiences. Some of them are very personal."

"I guess I did the right thing, for I never would have been so fortunate as to have met Hassan and you."

113

"Well, I understand how you feel about Hassan, but I'm just another guy trying to make my way in this tough world."

"No, I am really happy we have met, and I know good things will happen to us both."

He wanted to make sure she understood. "I would like to see that happen! It seems this new venture we are proposing will bring us closer together on all levels. I am the eternal optimist, and when I believe in a project or a person, it has my complete attention. You might get sick of me!"

He sensed that even though she had total loyalty to Hassan, something was not right. It was difficult to put his finger on it. If they were going to be close, it would work its way to the surface. Michael took her hands in his. She did not pull back.

"This Egyptian damsel wishes to go dancing. Are you game?" she said.

Michael got up and bowed. "Whatever thou wishest, my dear!" So off they went.

Doria wanted Michael to see a belly dancer. The club she brought him to had two shows a night, and the floor would be open for the patrons to dance. The art of belly dancing goes back to the time of the pharaohs. There were drawings on many of the tombs and temple walls depicting the importance, for they played an important part in ancient Egyptian rituals and celebrations. Modern-day belly dancers had blended folk, gypsy, and Ottoman together. It was considered an art and was at its best in Egypt.

Michael feigned surprise, as he had seen belly dancing in Tel Aviv. He did not want to ruin her supposed joke on him. He played the rite perfectly, stuffing an Egyptian pound note in her costume.

They had clasped hands and now they were on the dance floor close to one another. There was electricity, lots of kilowatts, between them. What they both had tried to control until then was gone. They both realized they were where they wanted to be: in each other's arms. There was little talk, just holding each other as the music ballads played on.

Joshua and Aron were having problems finding the two agents they needed to send to Michael. One of the candidates was in an auto accident and incapacitated. They needed a replacement who could pass as a production person. They searched their ranks, hoping to find someone with either experience or aptitude. To their surprise, the search came up with a name very familiar to them, Michael's good friend over a six-year period, Benjamin "Bengy" Barak. It was an unusual situation, and it raised a lot of questions as to whether this could work.

They brought Bengy in and went through the entire project. In a way, they liked the idea. The two understood one another, and trust was a serious issue in this type of situation. There certainly would be no problem working together. The more they thought about it and kicked it around with Bengy, they sold themselves on going ahead.

Aron had work to do setting up the same "cover" as they had with Michael. Sir Arthur was totally on board. He suggested that Bengy not only come to London to establish a pseudo-position but actually take a weeklong course in what he was supposed to accomplish in Egypt.

Bengy could not have been happier to be working with Michael. He felt the close relationship would be a plus in achieving the goal. There was communication between the Israelis and Michael. It was on the telex directly to Michael's office. They wanted to give him a heads-up about Bengy and did not want it to be a total surprise. All of this was playing out while Michael was on the dance floor.

The silence, as we say, was deafening. Both realized that they were in uncharted waters and they did not have life preservers. Doria felt if she succumbed to her emotions she would betray Hassan and all he had done for her. Michael realized if he took the next step, he was putting the whole plan in jeopardy. All he could think of was a quote, a line from a pop song: "Fools rush in where angels fear to tread."

Whatever immediate decisions they made would not bring the desired outcome for either party. The music was over and it was time to go.

Michael started to get silly, telling her stories. It created some space and allowed them to get their bearings. They had put out the burning fire, but the embers were still glowing in the darkness. Doria had planned to take him to see Giza the next day. She came by in the morning, and off they went.

Giza was the third-largest city in Egypt, located on the west bank of the Nile, southwest of central Cairo and a short ride away. It was famous, as it sat on the Giza Plateau, the site of the most impressive ancient monuments in the world. Included in this complex of ancient Egyptian structures were the Great Sphinx, the Great Pyramid of Giza, and a number of other large pyramids and temples. It was the focal point in Egypt's history due to its location close to Memphis, the ancient pharaonic capital of the Old Kingdom. It was the center of several conquests by the Persians, Greeks, Romans, and Byzantines. With the final conquest by the Muslims, the city was founded in 641 AD. It was named Al-Jizzah in Arabic, which meant "valley" or "plateau."

Giza, like Cairo, has a hot desert climate, and the drive there brought them into a windstorm, bringing the Saharan dust into play. It did not last long, and they both seemed excited to be together and looked forward to the experience. It was a popular place to live, for there were luxury apartments being built along the Nile with proximity to Cairo. There was a lot to see in one day. The views of the landscape before them were overwhelming. Michael had looked up the definition of a pyramid in an dictionary. "It is a solid figure with a polygonal base and triangular faces that meet a common point or a massive monument of ancient Egypt culminating in a single apex built over or around a crypt or tomb."

They hired a guide and horses. He was quite informative. "The word 'pyramid' actually comes from the Greek word 'pyramis,' which means 'wheat cake.' This word was used to describe the ancient Egyptian buildings because they reminded the Greeks of pointy-top wheat cakes."

They went to the Great Sphinx first. The guide was well-versed and knew his history. "The Sphinx was carved from a mound of natural rock. It was considered to be the 'guard' in front of Khafre's pyramid. Legends abound about the Great Sphinx. It was believed that it had powers and there were hidden passageways underneath. Nothing was ever found.

"There is a story of a young prince who fell asleep next to the Great Sphinx. It was written between its toes. He dreamt that the Sphinx promised him he would become the ruler of upper and lower Egypt if he cleared away the sand covering its body. The rest of the story is gone so you will have to use your imagination to work out the ending." They were arm in arm and laughed.

They moved on to the Great Pyramids. "The largest pyramid is known as the Great Pyramid. It took over twenty years to build with over on hundred thousand people working for three months each year during the Nile's annual flood when they could not farm the land. It was built with over 2.3 million limestone blocks, each weighing two and a half tons. The pyramid included burial chambers, a mortuary temple, and a causeway leading down to the Valley Temple. It was built by Pharaoh Khufu. In ancient times, the structure was considered one of the seven wonders of the world!"

They spent some additional time with the guide asking questions. Michael was curious about the stone and the technical construction, which was amazing. The lower layers were built of granite and the upper of gleaming white limestone, which had been stripped clean over the years.

Riding around the structures, they decided the day was too hot and they had enough of the wonders of the ancient world. By the time they returned to Cairo, they were famished, for they had forgone lunch. It was an interesting day and they enjoyed each other's company. They weren't running out of conversation and seemed to entertain one another. There was laughter and some serious talk about the state of the world. Michael wanted to get an idea of where she stood on her political views without being too inquisitive.

"Have you ever been involved in Egyptian politics?"

"Daniel, you seem to be either slightly naive or sarcastic. This is not the UK. It is a topic most people avoid, and I am one of them. Let's say that where I am in my life, it would not be wise to be on either side of the political situation."

It was early for dinner, so they again went to a café for drinks. Doria was full of smiles. "I have a surprise for you. Tomorrow we are going to Sharm El Sheikh. We will stay two nights. I have booked a two-bedroom suite in a great hotel. You need the sun and the sea, and I do too. I don't know if you have a swimsuit, but if not, you can buy one there. We will be beachcombers for two days and have a real break. I don't know about you, but I need it badly!"

"My God, what could be better!"

"We will meet at the airport early and we will be there in no time, for it's a short flight. I do not want to drive three hundred miles. I want the time at the beach. Here is your ticket before I lose it."

Chapter Sixteen

Michael threw a few things into his bag and was ready to go. He had gym shorts and sneakers, which would do until he shopped for some other items. Jeans, shorts, and a linen jacket would be the attire while they were there.

He had gone to the office after dinner and sent a telex to Fantastique to let them know about his journey and where he was staying. He did not mention Doria. That was his private domain. They did not have to know his every move. On second thought, he wanted them to know where he was, but it was not necessary to know who he was with, at least for now.

Sharm El Sheikh sits over the Straits of the Kings of Tiran at the mouth of the Gulf of Aqaba and near the Red Sea. In fact, it's called part of the Red Sea Riviera. It's the perfect spot for sun, sand, and scuba diving, and the perfect choice to ease the stress of both he and Doria.

Doria booked a good hotel run by Italians that had a five-star restaurant that your mother would be proud of. They arrived before noon and found Michael a bathing suit and some T-shirts. Doria had brought tanning lotion and two pair of goggles.

The suite was perfect, with a sitting room between the two bedrooms. Michael was apprehensive as to whether he could keep his hands off her. He was not made of wood, and there was more on his mind than "just a roll in the hay." There were serious feelings building in his mind and body.

Michael was excited. "Let's go to the beach. I can't wait to get in the water."

There were very few places on earth where scuba diving and water sports reached this level. Snorkeling, diving, and windsurfing were all activities that were perfect for the Red Sea Riviera. The underwater scenery was magnificent. They had beach lounges and an umbrella set up. Doria had come down wearing a robe, sort of a see-through cover-up. When they reached the beach, she took it off. Michael could not take his eyes off her. Doria's figure was, one would say, memorable . . . just flawless.

"Daniel, turn around. I want to put some oil on your back. You will burn to a crisp. This sun is brutal."

She was wearing a one-piece black suit that was simple and classic but could not have been sexier. It was the woman in it who generated sensuous thoughts. They decided to sit under the umbrella until the heat got to them. Then, the sea would beckon them. The lounges were quite close together with a small table placed between them. Michael did not stop talking, for he was afraid if he did, he would lose his poise and take her in his arms. Finally, he calmed down and was able to contain himself.

"Doria, we have known each other just over three weeks, and here we are on vacation. I like the program—work two weeks and then sneak away to paradise."

She laughed. "That would be a wonderful way to exist, at least for a few months. I imagine you would get bored with me and find another situation."

"Bored with you! That's highly unlikely. You have all these wonderful traits. You are a great travel agent, know all the good restaurants, and are a beautiful tour guide. What more could I want? Oh, by the way, you dance very well!"

"I am so happy you recognize all my qualities. I guess that means I'm assured of at least an additional two weeks!" They laughed.

They would have lunch on the beach after a quick swim. The water was magnificent, not as refreshing as the North Shore of Boston or the Cape. There was a raft set up about forty feet from the beach, and they both headed for it. Michael lay on the raft. Doria was still in the sea treading water, her head close to the edge of the raft where Michael lay. She bobbed in the water and they spoke with one another.

"Michael, tell me more about you. I am so curious about your life and family."

He was at odds with himself. There wasn't much choice but to give her the "party line." What he did do was weave as much truth as possible into the story.

"Doria, my dream is to make a life for myself in the States, where I went to school. My heritage, as yours, is without a question here in the Middle East. I have another heritage made in the New World, the USA. I spent considerable time in New England. It is so different from what I have seen in my limited travels. It's like the UK, originally settled by English people seeking peace and wanting to practice their way of life. England is where I live, but it is America that beckons me."

"I understand what you are saying. My life here in Egypt is quite good. I have seen the UK and admire what they have done. I told you the stories of my father's experiences in America. We are coming of age here. Arab nationalism is the center of our attention and our dreams. The question is: are we on the right track? President Nasser has taken us on a mission to make Egypt great and bring back the dignity it once experienced. The goal is to restore our place in the world of nations. I am not happy with some of his methods or plans of action. But he has done quite a bit to make Egypt better, especially for women."

"When you say you are unhappy with some of his methods, what do you mean?"

"War is not the answer. It never is. I am not happy with our alliance with Syria or a United Arab Republic. I am certainly not in accord with our involvement in Yemen. It was horrible. The expulsion of foreign nationals and Jews is not what I personally stand for."

She had had enough of the sea, turning and swimming back to the beach. Michael followed, diving into the water wondering where all this conversation was leading. He raced her to the beach.

He had to be on his toes, for he wanted to tell her who he was and why he was there. Yet Michael wanted to draw her out and hear what she had to say. They toweled themselves and each other, laughing about who beat who in the race to the beach.

"I said these things to you when we were alone in the water. This is not the UK or the USA. One must be careful what is said in public."

The beach was not crowded. It was midweek, and there were only a handful of mostly foreigners under umbrellas. They decided to walk, for the beach was endless. Letting the tide run through their toes was delightful. There really wasn't a choice, for the sand was a cauldron of heat. The sifting sand at their feet felt great as they enjoyed the warm tide.

Michael took her by both hands and twirled her around and around, letting the surf splash on her body. There was a slight resistance, but almost immediately it was gone. She was enjoying the ride. They must have walked a mile or two. When they looked back, they could not make out the hotel. They sat down in the water, their lower bodies awash in the tide.

"Daniel, I can't begin to tell you how much I am enjoying this break. It is beyond my expectations."

"My dear, as a British gentleman, it is my duty to be your 'champion' and deliver every wish you desire."

"Well, Sir Daniel, I would not expect less. You may be my champion as long as you are able to deliver sunshine, surf, and enough suntan lotion on my back!"

The conversation turned more serious. "Tell me, Doria, I do not want to pry into Hassan's business dealings that have no relationship with Fantastique, but what are all these Germans doing? Please don't answer if it is a problem."

"I was waiting for you to ask me. First of all, they are, for the most part, working for Nasser and the government. I am not privy to their projects, although I know they are involved in technical developments of all kinds. They are also involved in training the military. I do not have any real contact with them except on communicating with Germany. They all speak English and some Arabic, so arranging travel plans is not an issue. I really don't know how much Hassan is involved with them. His relationship with Nasser is entirely different. They are thick as thieves. They have a business and personal relationship, and I believe they are related in some way. I would suggest that you have little to do with them. The Germans, as you, have their own suites and there's a common dining room. I have arranged for you to have dinners brought to your room. As you know, there are sections of the complex that are strictly off-limits to you and your techs. These are not Hassan's or my rules but stem from the Egyptian government and are enforced by their security forces that are on-site. That is not entirely true. Hassan does not want you to be in any way involved in his business activities and forbids your access to the rest of the complex outside of EgyptCo. Let's leave it like this."

Michael acknowledged her remarks. "I shall live by the rules."

He wanted to hear more from her, but this had to happen at her pace. They decided to walk back and played tag, running in and out of the water. Michael took her by the hand. She was smiling.

"So who do you want to be when you grow up?"

Michael was smiling.

"I always wanted to be a fireman until I was five or six. Then, an artist. I guess that really hasn't changed. My world is art, fashion, and probably, more important, doing my best. I try to give the maximum effort in everything.

"Actually, when you do your best, in that way there are no regrets. Whatever I attempted in my life, I have always given my all. In my experiences, it has always been staying power that led to success. I guess I would like to live my life in the words of Winston Churchill: 'Success is not final, failure not fatal. It is the courage to continue that counts.'"

"And what is your objective with me?"

He smiled. "'Objective' is not a word I would use. Goals would be a far better word. That's an interesting question. There are a number of goals I would like to achieve. Number one, I want us to be true friends. Number two, I want to see our business relations realized without serious issues. Number three, I want you to find the answers to all the questions you have in your life. Number four . . . I guess that's a work in progress. I will use your word 'objective' in this instance. You seem to want a definitive answer, and that's not possible now. I feel you and I have reached a pivotal point in our relationship. It is now more personal, and the ultimate goal or objective is still elusive. There are factors in play that need to be defined only in time. I guess that's not exactly clear, but at least it sounds right."

Doria looked at him. "Is that where we are? It seems we are in the hands of the gods."

"Can you tell me which ones, so I won't dilly-dally around with the wrong ones."

It was the perfect rebuttal and broke them both up! The day was fading, and they had had enough of the sun and sand, which was in all their things.

Michael took her by the arm and led her to the veranda. "Let's have a drink or possibly two and sit on the terrace."

Michael ran to his room and changed his shirt but still stayed in his suit. Doria just wrapped herself in her robe.

"Why is it that I feel guilty being here instead of working away?"

Michael was boisterous. "Probably because you were 'strongarmed' and stolen away to be with me. It sounds plausible. At least it has the ring of authenticity. They taught me at Harvard Business School whenever you are in this type of situation, lay back and enjoy it. That lesson, my dear, cost over $75,000 in tuition fees!"

The conversation turned to business, and they discussed how Michael would proceed in establishing the necessary pieces of the operation to produce the "right" product.

"I would hope we will see the patterns from the UK upon our return."

CHAPTER SEVENTEEN

ARON AND JOSHUA ACCOMPANIED THE TWO TECHNICIANS to London. Sir Arthur had made plans to give them a "crash course" in their presumed positions. Bengy and Avrom spent over a week, fourteen hours a day, gaining an expertise level that would be adequate. Meanwhile, the boys had dispatched their Egyptian contact to Sharm El Sheikh to check on Mr. Amin. They weren't spying on him, nor was it a protective issue. They just wanted to know what was occurring. Big brother was always watching you.

Doria and Michael went upstairs to shower and change. There were two separate bedrooms but only one shower. Doria went first. He could hear her singing as the sound of the water mingled with the words. He wanted to part the curtains and jump in. He just didn't have the balls to do it. Yet he felt that he would not be met with opposition. Doria was more than interested. At least that was his impression. What the evening would bring created a sense of excitement, mystery, and the feeling that he was about to enter an adventure that he had never dreamt of or experienced.

He let the water cascade over his head as he fantasized her being in his arms. The hot water was soothing to his skin as he soaped himself for a final rinse. He didn't hear the curtains part or feel a body take a position behind him. All of a sudden, he felt her. She clasped her hands around his neck and pulled her body toward him.

Michael was just so caught off guard and stunned to find this wonderful creature wanting him. He pulled her around and kissed her with all his strength. The water was there, but her lips were so luscious, delightful, so willing. He could hardly believe what was happening. His hands were everywhere and so were hers. Michael had her legs around his waist and entered her. The water continued to cascade and they clung to one another until they climaxed. Her passion showed in every movement, and he could not stop caressing her. They sat down and the water continued to fall over them both. They finally arose and found the Turkish towel robes provided. They slipped them on and drew each other to the bedroom.

They were there for what seemed like hours, entwined, watching the light recede to darkness. Not many words were spoken. There was not a need. As the night descended, they clung to each other, afraid it was only a dream.

"I think we understand each other but, tell me, do you always invite yourself into somebody else's shower?"

"I said to myself: 'This guy is going to wine and dine me, fill me with champagne, and carry me off to bed.' I wanted to make sure he washed himself properly!" They were both hysterical.

"I really don't know what came over me. We both have been looking at one another with 'I want you' written over our faces. I thought this was the right time."

"Let me say that I never was so shocked in my life when I felt your arms around me. Just to set the record straight, I had already washed properly!" They burst out laughing.

Dinner was Italian, and Michael was famished. He had veal and pasta while Doria just had the pasta dish. They lingered over coffee and dessert, hand over hand, across the table. They couldn't take their eyes off each other. Their legs were entangled under the table.

"Let's take a walk after dinner. Not too long, for we have unfinished business to attend to." Again, smiles!

They lay in each other's arms trying to convey their feelings in every way possible. Michael felt this was not just another "conquest." This had brought on feelings that he had never experienced. Doria told him she had felt this special bond almost immediately upon their meeting one another. Love at first sight was pretty close to an explanation for them both. They fell asleep in each other's arms to awake later, full of passion for one another. Both were in fine physical shape, and what they were attempting to achieve could come close to sexual records in stamina and style.

They had another day before returning to the real world, and they tried to make the most of it, wanting again to know everything about each other. Michael realized that he was at a disadvantage but could not divulge the true situation. They had spoken earlier, and he mixed the truth with his cover story as best he could.

They didn't want to get any more sun, so they stayed under the umbrella. In fact, they got another one to give maximum shade. Doria wanted to talk. She really didn't hold back much about herself or her family. Hassan came up in the conversation, and she wanted Michael to know exactly where she stood with him. There wasn't a personal or sexual relationship. In fact, she thought Hassan could be gay. This was a very difficult situation to deal with for a Muslim living in Egypt. Homosexuality was considered a crime in Egypt, and you were ostracized by the community. Doria did not want to brand him as one, as he had been married, but her instincts told her he was gay. He had a life in Germany that she knew nothing about.

There were times when she felt there were events going on that were not benefitting Egypt or the world.

She talked in depth about his relationship with Nasser. Not only were they personally close, but they were in business together. She knew he was in the munitions business but had no idea to what degree. She thought it only was to help Nasser and Egypt.

She hesitated and then spoke. "Hassan's relationship with Nasser is really intertwined. I believe they are partners in a number of ventures that run from real estate to a munitions corporation. Hassan set up a separate corporation with him on all munitions and chemical sales to Egypt. In that way, Nasser has income from these sales.

"There are other business deals they are involved in together that are part of their involvement in Syria, which I know nothing about. This all started when Nasser brought about Syria's part in the UAR. Nasser's wife's family seems to be heavily involved. I know Nasser would like to diversify his assets and have some in Germany with Hassan. He has put pressure on Hassan to become part of his European business."

Her knowledge of the German/Swiss dealings was negligible. He kept that part of his operation completely separate from Cairo. She was told to cooperate in every way with Michael. Hassan felt that a successful story with Fantastique would open the world apparel industry to EgyptCo. They had a once-in-a-lifetime opportunity to develop this business.

"He was suspicious of you in the initial meetings but now has every confidence that you are working to make this program successful."

As far as her work was concerned, she was a communications expert and made sure all was running well. She surprised Michael by telling him that she spoke German. It made sense since she communicated with Hassan's offices in Munich almost daily.

As a Director of EgyptCo, she managed the administrative end of the business and had the power to deal with the agencies worldwide that sold the goods. The program that Michael was proposing would be a major step forward for her if it were successful. But that was not her ultimate goal. She was not happy with what was happening in Egypt. Nasser was a dictator, and she saw the influence of German and ex-Nazi thinking developing in her country. She did not understand deporting foreign residents and Jews. She had said this to Michael when they talked in Cairo. But now it was more emphatic and came from her heart. Michael felt that she was bearing her soul.

He said very little that morning but listened and tried to keep things in perspective regarding the course of the events that were to follow, unleashed by his hand.

They took a quick swim. Michael couldn't keep his hands off her and had her bathing suit off in the deep water. It was sheer paradise for them both. They took lunch on the patio where it was shaded by a tent-like covering. There was a breeze, but it was from the desert. Lunch brought some small talk, and they discussed the afternoon's activities. They drank wine and toasted themselves. The consensus was to take a siesta, and they went to their suite. They laughed and joked over the shower experience.

Laying on the bed naked in each other's arms, they were content being intertwined. They slept two hours and awakened refreshed, deciding to shower. Only this time they turned the water on together. Laziness overcame them, for they had no other wish than to be with one another. Again sitting on the patio, they drank prosecco and talked until the sun was dropping into the sea. The more the day went on, the more Michael was concerned about how to proceed with the events that had occurred. This was not just lust for each other. It was a unique discovery of a person you love. There was so much to say and there wasn't a possibility of his talking about what was to happen. It was in his every thought.

Michael commented, "When we get back to reality, how are we going to proceed? I am not able to come up with any answer that will work for us both. I do not want to lie, but at the same time, I am not sure how all this will 'fly' with Hassan. I realize when we see him he is not going to interrogate us, but he will ask questions. How should we proceed?"

Doria summed it up: "I am more vulnerable than you. Hassan will not look favorably on knowing of our relationship. As far as I'm concerned, we had a wonderful two days and it was strictly platonic in every way. I have to approach it in this manner. I have no choice in the short term but to lie."

Michael felt good at what he heard. As far as he was concerned, it was the only course of action.

Over dinner they discussed how they were going to work together and, most important, spend time with one another. Michael thought the best way to meet would be at his Cairo apartment on the weekends or when it was necessary for him to be in the city. He gave her a key, and she would be able to arrive before him if necessary. During the week, they would be at the complex, but it would be difficult and not very smart to have any sort of relationship except a business one. This solved their being together temporarily but did not address the real problem.

He did not know what would be her reaction to the destruction of Hassan. Somehow, he had to make her understand. She had expressed concern over Hassan's munitions business and Nasser's ambition of extreme nationalism and conquest. There was hope.

They slept soundly after making love, so softly, so innocently. There was passion in every movement, a sense of losing one another if any part of their bodies were not enjoined.

The morning sun sneaked through the shutters as they dressed. The return to Cairo brought a totally different outlook.

CHAPTER EIGHTEEN

ARON AND JOSHUA SIGNED OFF ON BENGY AND AVROM. They were pleased with their week in London.

Sir Arthur thought they had gained more than a working knowledge of their positions. He was amazed at their ability and competence. "If you decide on a career change, please come back and see me."

Their cover was intact, and both men felt they were not at a disadvantage. In fact, they thought their ability to adapt to situations was their strength.

With Doria's help, Michael moved into the complex. He received notification that his guys would be arriving in two days with the initial patterns that would get the product development started. In the meantime, his priority was to learn all about Hassan's operation. He needed input from Doria, but that had to be handled very carefully. There was only so much he could ask. Being in the complex gave him the opportunity to explore and learn about his fellow boarders. They worked in another area, but everyone ate together, so there was a great opportunity to find the answers he needed.

Hannah was concerned about Michael even though he told her that communication would be difficult over the next four to five weeks. She sensed there was more to his explanation than he was saying, but there wasn't much she could do about it. She had Bengy's number but did not want to call. She spoke with Abe and Sarah on a regular basis, and they kept telling her that Michael needed the break. He had put in six years of nonstop work, both academically and working with them. They wanted him back, as he was a key player, not only for the future, but he was an important cog in the everyday business. She always felt better when they spoke. In fact, they were going to have dinner together, which would put her even more at ease. She was also pleased with the course of Michael's life. He was on his way to having everything she wished for him and more. Hannah knew Michael needed the time away from all that was going on in his life. However, they were not happy with the lack of contact with him. If they didn't hear from him soon, calling Israel would be an option. They were major donors and had some pull at the government level. Abe was willing to wait a reasonable length of time before calling.

Bengy and Avrom arrived late in the evening and Michael met them. He had made hotel reservations for them for three nights. After that, they would relocate to the complex with him. Michael wanted to have some time with them away from Doria, Hassan, and the staff.

They went through customs and immigration without a problem. Michael didn't know if Hassan had sent anyone to view their arrival. All parties handled it well. He had his driver take them to the hotel and made a breakfast date for the next day. There were few words between them. They would have time over the next two days to put their plan together.

Michael was right about playing it straight. Hassan had sent his service to see them arrive and to photograph both technicians as well as Michael. They reported back to him the following morning with their impression of the arrivals.

Michael met them in the hotel lobby and brought them to his office after breakfast. He had not spent any real time here, so the three of them went through the office looking for any listening devices. Then Michael embraced them both and got down to business.

Bengy began the conversation. He gave Michael an update from the boys and their week in London. He and Avrom gave him a rundown on what was happening in Israel and the world in general. Michael laid out the plan on the blackboard, step by step. Each point was discussed in detail.

"Guys, we will be living in their complex, which houses not only EgyptCo, where we will be working on the development of their apparel business, but also their munitions operations. They are warehoused there and administered in the same area. Doria runs the apparel and bedsheets division for Hassan and is also his communications person here in Egypt."

Bengy spoke up. "Michael, or should I say Daniel, we have just arrived and are totally dependent on your picture of the situation. You have given us the basic facts. We need more."

"She's a bright, beautiful woman and Hassan's right hand in this area of his business. As far as I can tell, she has no connection with the munitions and chemicals. Time will tell if I am wrong, but for now, let's see what happens. We need to remember that Hassan was raised and educated in Germany and Switzerland, so we are not dealing with just an Arabic mentality. It is cold, calculating Teutonic superiority that faces us. On top of that is his hatred of Israel. He is totally involved in the Rocket Project with Nasser. We know Hassan's and Nasser's goal is to rain down rockets on Israel developed by these Nazi scientists As the main importer of all the components,

136

he is vital to Nasser's project. We must destroy his ability to supply the program.

"Bengy, or should I say Mr. Clark, that brings us to these Nazi bastards they brought from Germany and South America. They are scientists and munitions experts. Our main concern is those involved in the Rocket Program. We will be living with them and probably spending some time with them in the evenings. We will definitely see them at dinner. We want to identify the key personnel for Tel Aviv. I don't know how much information we will be able to put together, but we will be in their midst. Both of you speak German, so we need to decide whether you speak to them or just listen. Let's table that for the moment."

Bengy and Avrom nodded in agreement. Michael continued, "Now, let's talk about our cover. Both of you are supposed to be involved in setting up the production and quality control. They do not have a production line capable of making garments, mainly women's shirts or cotton sportswear. What is in our favor is that the time it will take to develop sample product should be sufficient for us to complete our mission. So in my estimation, it would be extremely difficult to expose your inexperience in a project that is just getting started."

Bengy spoke up. "Michael, we can't stand around and watch you."

"Both of you will look for stitchers and cutters for the production line. You are more than capable of knowing what to do after your time in London. So you will be busy while I work on developing the samples. That should be our plan in this area. I'm sure you will be able to pull it off. I see you have the patterns that I requested, so we will get started on that basis.

"Let's discuss what we are ready to do here. We will probably move in tomorrow or the next day, depending on our getting everything done. We won't be able to have any serious conversations there. I'm not sure if the rooms are wired, but I really don't even want to go about checking them out in any way. We have to presume they are and act accordingly.

"Our main objective is to pinpoint the two areas in the complex that comprise the heart of his operation. Number one, we want to destroy his inventory and warehouse operation. Number two, we want to wipe out the Rocket research and development section, thereby destroying it permanently. Number three, we want to identify as many Nazis as possible.

"Summing this up, we are not sure how to proceed with the final plan to reduce his operations to rubble. When we identify the exact location, the decision will be made. The choices are an attack by air or setting explosive charges. Our communications to Tel Aviv will dictate the choice. I believe it will depend on whether we are able to ensure our ability to leave the scene. This is not a suicide mission. The research area falls under the same scenario. As far as the Nazis are concerned, our identification of them will go a long way in ending their ability to work in this program."

Michael continued, "We have been invited to dinner with Doria and Hassan. You will get to meet them both and will have a better idea of who they are. We will have lunch here. I can place a takeout order. I want to just go over all our thoughts again and hear what you have to say. I'll take you back to the hotel and let you nap for a few hours before dinner. We want to be at our best for them both. I have a meeting in the late afternoon with the fashion school regarding a pattern maker. Now that we have the patterns, I can get them started with the training program. After lunch, I will tell you more about that segment of the operation. Before we eat, tell me about what's happening in this crazy world. I read yesterday's *Herald Tribune* and the pro-Nasser *Daily*. I'll tell you more about Hassan and Doria. Don't get any ideas about Doria. If anybody is in line, I am!" They all laughed. They didn't realize Michael was telling the truth.

Dinner that evening went pretty much according to the script. Hassan and Doria hosted the threesome at what was probably the finest restaurant in Cairo. Everyone seemed to be enjoying themselves. Hassan's English was excellent. Bengy and Avrom both had strong English accents, being educated in Israel under the British educational system.

Hassan asked questions, and both the boys answered them without a hitch. Doria kept the conversation on the light side, offering her services to make their stay enjoyable. She proposed local tours on the weekend and some other places they might want to visit.

Michael had not seen Doria since they returned from Sharm El Sheikh. She was radiant and ever so beautiful as she played the hostess role. He could feel her presence and had to do everything possible not to stare at her.

Hassan directed his question to Michael: "When are we going to get started? I am excited and impatient to see this project become a reality. I realize you and Fantastique have made a major commitment to build this business with me. I am completely at your service for whatever resources you need."

Michael answered, "We will be moving to the complex the day after tomorrow. We need another day to work out the schedule and the use of the fashion school for pattern making. Mr. Clark will start interviewing workers after they have been to the factory. We are on our way."

Chapter Nineteen

Hassan dropped them at the hotel. Michael said he wanted to have a nightcap with the boys and would find his way home. They all were pleased with the way the evening went. Michael wanted to show anyone watching that the three "Englishmen" were very real.

When he returned to his apartment he was tired but content that all seemed to be working out. Michael threw his jacket on the couch as he walked into the dark bedroom in deep thought. He started to disrobe. Sitting on the edge, he slipped off his shoes and socks. He was about to go into the bathroom when those magical hands surrounded his shoulders and caressed his body. He was totally surprised and immediately responded to her warm body. Who was this magical woman who had captivated him? Who was this woman he could not resist and, at the same time, radiated danger for them both? There was nothing to say. Love was the act and thoughts of the moment.

"Daniel, if I did not see you now, I do not know when we would have another opportunity. I can't believe that I am doing this and that I initiated this lovemaking by jumping in the shower. Yet here I am loving you. Tell me, Daniel. Am I worthy of you? Have you respect for me? Have I done something wrong? What have I done? I just could not help myself!"

Michael hugged her. "My love, I cannot tell you that I wasn't surprised—no, shocked—to feel you in the shower. But we both know that we were overtaken with one another. I have never experienced anything like our meeting and knowing one another. This does not happen every day. Our getting together seemed to be willed by our mutual desire for one another. It is a blending of our souls that is happening. I can't think of it in any other way. You are part of me. The test of time will tell the story!"

It was early morning, and they lay in each other's arms not knowing what to say to each other. Words were not necessary.

"Doria, I believe it's better if I leave first. I have to meet them for breakfast, and you will not be noticed in the morning commute.

They spent another day going over the checklist, and he brought them to the fashion school to view the pattern people. They were ready to move in the following morning.

Aron and Joshua got the report from their man in Egypt. He had been to Sharm El Sheikh and had seen Doria and Michael. His notes gave an accurate interpretation of the events. They gave him new marching orders.

They all moved their gear and made an in-depth walk through the facility. Doria became the tour director. She had made arrangements to interview workers for the project. The boys started to meet with the applicants. Michael now had the patterns from London and sat down with the staff to start working on developing samples.

He had more of a working knowledge of the complex. Although the apparel building was not attached to the rest of the structures, he believed the buildings next door housed the munitions warehouses. They were set up differently, as all the windows were shuttered and the building had been revamped so large trucks could be brought

141

directly into the structures. He believed each warehouse was just one floor with thirty-foot ceilings. He came to these conclusions by what he saw during his time on the factory floor. There were periods when the doors to both facilities were open to help with the heat of the day.

How many warehouses were involved was hard to say. All his discoveries made him believe that there were more than what they originally thought. It was a massive operation. Could they come up with a plan to accurately confirm the number of warehouses and their exact locations? That was the major question that needed an answer.

They had worked out a strategy at dinner. Michael and Avrom would speak to each other in English. Bengy would converse with the Nazis in German. His cover was that his parents were from Switzerland and moved to the UK before the war. German was actually his mother's tongue. The three of them tried to be as friendly as possible with their dinner companions, hoping to gain as much information as possible.

Michael picked up his conversation with the two ex-Nazis he had met at the club over the billiards table. They seemed cordial enough and were more than willing to engage him in conversation.

"Mr. Amin, I see you are starting an apparel operation for Mr. Hassan Streiger. It should be an interesting project. I wish you the very best."

"Thank you. My company, Fantastique, has made a major commitment to develop this business. What are you gentlemen doing here?"

"We are involved in a much different business than you. Let me say we are in the fireworks business in a way." There was laughter.

"We are working for the Egyptian government to develop their munitions and chemical industries. We are scientists with different skills but all in these areas. What's more important: do you play chess or billiards? Karl and I are looking desperately for anyone who can play."

Michael smiled. "I am more than available; just tell me when."

The chess pieces and board came out of nowhere.

"I hope I am decent competition. Tell me, how long have you been here?"

Alex was more than helpful.

"It's been about eight months, and we are here until the projects are completed. It is, as you say, open-ended. I am more interested in returning to Argentina as soon as possible."

Michael continued the conversation. "I don't know how long we will be here. It is a start-up, and that, as you say, is open-ended. It seems things are a bit limited around here. Is there an area where we can do some exercise? It is confining!"

Alex replied, "Let me show you in the morning. I like to get out there and work out most mornings. I'll meet you here at 6:30 a.m. Do you have gym clothes?"

"No problem. By the way, checkmate!" They patted each other on the shoulders. Michael had made significant headway.

The exercise yard was situated just in front of what he thought was the balance of the munitions warehouses. There was a series of at least five facilities, possibly one additional. Naturally, the area was fenced off from the buildings, but the fence was not electrified and probably could be climbed. Doria never showed him this in his tour, and he wondered why. He made a mental note to ask her.

He could now plan a late evening walk and get into the area after dark. Michael needed to know more about the security schedule. The major security was on the outside perimeter, and that played into his plans. Once you were inside, you were not a suspect. They were now part of Hassan's organization, so there was more of a relaxed presence.

Michael wanted to gain the confidence of Hassan. He and the team set up a small prototype line on the floor of the factory that made cotton sheets. It was adjacent to the area where they were weaving the cotton. Hassan was ecstatic seeing the production line coming to life. The project was showing signs of progress. With the help of the fashion school, they produced the first products. They were just samples, but there was significant headway being made. They were reaching Fantastique's standards slowly. The progress even surprised Michael. He realized he had made a breakthrough, and although it was not the major reason for being here, he was proud of the accomplishment. Hassan and Doria were shown the new prototypes, and both were excited to see progress. Michael was not sold on Hassan's total involvement developing this business. This step forward possibly changed his attitude, for he was hard to read. He only saw Doria for a few moments each day. There wasn't a chance to talk, and he avoided any real contact with her.

As far as the Fantastique program was concerned, they were on track. Bengy and Avrom had located a good portion of the work force they needed for the first limited production. It was mainly cutters and stitchers. They had brought training manuals with them and didn't have any problem developing the programs. Hassan had purchased the latest sewing machines and necessary equipment for cutting. They were sitting there in the original crates for quite some time.

Aron and Joshua were more than concerned about the course of events and were thinking of calling Michael back to London. They knew about Doria and presumed there was a possibility Michael was compromised. They could have him return to London on the pretext of a special meeting or event he could not miss. It would not be uncommon for management to request his presence. The consensus was to bring him back for three days.

When Michael received the news, he was somewhat concerned and thought they had come up with an alternative plan. He was slightly perplexed but knew something was up. They would only call him back for something urgent.

Michael wanted to see Doria before he left for London. It was not just for a night of lovemaking. He wanted certain information and had to see where he stood with Hassan. He had questions.

Bengy and Avrom would be staying. This was not an issue. They had worked out perfectly handling their part of the plan. The trio went to the fashion academy under the pretense of working with the patterns. They were able to get together in their office and go over details. What was needed was more accurate information on the exact location of each warehouse and the research facilities. They would work on getting this done while Michael was gone. The key point he made was not to take unnecessary chances.

Michael summarized the situation with Bengy and Avrom. "I will be gone only three to four days if the flights are on time. The boys need information, and we need to fill them in."

When Michael returned to Cairo, Doria was there in the apartment. He could see that she was visibly upset. "Why are you going back to London? Hassan and I are concerned that management has lost confidence in the project. Are they calling you back to shut it down?"

"Don't be silly. I'm returning for an executive corporate meeting. I will only be gone a few days. We haven't had a chance to talk about anything, including our personal relationship. I was under the impression that both of you were pleased with the prototypes we showed you a day ago. I still get the impression that Hassan is really not sold on us or the project."

"Daniel, that is not true. Hassan may have felt that way earlier but not now. He is totally committed. What's wrong?"

He had anger in his voice. "When you gave me a tour around the complex, you omitted showing me the exercise area."

"I was told not to. Hassan was still checking on you through his and Nasser's security people. He wanted to see if you were here to scrutinize all his operations. That area leads to the restricted zone."

"Why didn't you tell me this earlier?"

"I wanted to but was not sure how to proceed."

"We are more than lovers; at least those are my feelings. How could you not have told me?"

"You have to understand that as much as I love you, there is an allegiance to one's employer, especially if he has given you the opportunity of a lifetime. I felt it was a temporary situation, and I was right. He has total confidence in you."

Michael sighed. "So where do you stand?"

"I am desperately in love with you and want with all my heart a life with you. I realize this has been a whirlwind romance. It has caught me totally by surprise. Again, I can't believe that I was the aggressor, jumping in the shower. You have turned my world totally upside down. Somehow or another, I feel there is more to this whole affair than I can understand. It is nothing I can put my hands around, but I sense there is more and I am afraid for you. I don't know why I feel that way. It is frightening, and I do not know what to do."

Michael took her in his arms and pleaded with her to stop sobbing. "We are both in a difficult situation. Suddenly, I find myself in love with this Egyptian goddess. What have I gotten myself into? What has occurred to create your fear for me?"

"As I said, there isn't any particular reason. You are in Egypt under the control of Nasser's security forces and Hassan's organization. If anything goes wrong, you will be subject to their wrath. I have seen their 'displeasure' in action. It is not pretty."

Michael prodded her for an answer. "Again, I ask the question; why do you feel this way? There has to be something that makes you suspicious."

Doria became very serious. "My love, when we were in Sharm El Sheikh, you were very restless during the night. I couldn't make out much of what you were saying, but you did mention Nazis and rockets. You were dreaming, and it was only for a moment. Who is Hannah?"

Michael looked at her. "Hannah is my mother, who reminds me of you. She is an unbelievable woman who raised me without my father, who died early. It is a long story for another time. As for what you heard me say, why didn't you tell this story to Hassan?"

"My God, why would you say that? That is the last person in the world I would tell. Don't you realize that I love you and would do anything in the world to protect you? What is going on? I must know. It is unfair to keep me in the dark."

Michael pushed his hair back, hesitating. "Doria, I am putting my life and probably the lives of a lot of other people in your hands. Are you prepared to hear who I really am?"

"What do you mean?"

"My real name is Michael Janssen." He told her his life story. He left nothing out—his ancestry, his education, the story of his dad and his hatred of the Nazis. He told her of working for the Israelis and why he was doing so.

"The world of Hassan and Nasser has to be stopped, even destroyed. They will not be allowed to hurt my people and create havoc here in Egypt, the Middle East, and throughout the world.

"Hassan is fueling revolutions, supplying terrorists, creating dictators with his munitions. He is bringing to Nasser the means to develop V-2 rockets that will be used against Israel and others who oppose Pan-Arab nationalism. You have been part of these plans, whether you realize it or not. You have been 'branded' as part of the organization. In the eyes of those of us who oppose this, you are the enemy. Is this where you want to be? Is this what you stand for? So I ask you: now that you know my story and my interpretation of events and my desire to stop this insanity, where are you in this mess?"

Doria did not hesitate. "I am with you in every way. Not because I love you, which happens to be a major commitment on my part. I have been extremely concerned about the work that Hassan has been involved with through his munitions business. Nasser working with ex-Nazis to develop rockets is not what Egypt needs. In my opinion, he has become a tyrant and is leading the Egyptian people on a destructive course ending in ruin. As far as Israel is concerned, they have a right to exist. The Jewish people have suffered enough at the hands of the Nazis. I have no quarrel with the Jews or the Israelis. We have no right to continue aggression toward them. Now, where does that put me in this whole affair?"

Michael held her hand.

She said, "I know what is going through your head. 'Can I, can they, trust her? Will she expose our plans? What shall we do?' I would be asking the same questions that are going through your head."

Michael replied, "Yes, now you have been brought into this dangerous situation because of our love for each other. The decision to be one of us cannot just be based on love. It has to be a desire to stand for all that is right, the good of mankind. There has to be a core belief that goes to the heart of one's convictions."

Doria had tears in her eyes. "I am willing to be with you in every way. Not only because I love you, but I believe in what you are doing and what is right. I realize what I am saying is a commitment forever. I love you, Michael, and what you stand for."

Michael was also crying. They were tears not only of joy but of admiration and pride in her. He could not control himself as they embraced. They sat together and tried to comprehend everything that had happened.

"Doria, I am off to London and will have to tell my people about you. I cannot hide it from them. They will want to know everything. We are now in this together. I did not want to involve you, but it just happened. There are two alternatives. I can go to London and resign from the mission. Bengy and Avrom will come back and they will formulate another plan. You can go on with your working with Hassan. What you decide to do, I will leave up to you.

"The other option is to join us. I do not have to tell you how dangerous this will be. The question is: can you honestly believe that you are not a traitor but rather working to keep Egypt from the hands of the Nazis and a man who desires to be a dictator? I do not know if this is possible for you to transpose yourself into this being. If you can't, I understand. I do not know if I could do it. I am relieved that

149

I'm not put in this position. Whatever your answer is, it cannot be based on just loving me. It must be a lot more than just what we mean to each other. Your decision has all kinds of repercussions that will affect my life and those of many others."

"Michael, I want to call you by your real name here in the confines of this apartment. My life until now has not been challenged. What I mean by that is I have never had to stand up for my beliefs. They have fallen into place, mainly through the course of events. My political views have always been liberal, leaning usually left of center. The tenets of what I stand for have not really been tested because there was never any need to do so. I went along, for lack of better words, 'with the tides.' It was easy and it worked. This thinking brought me relative success, which manifested itself in my current position. A woman's ability to become a director of a significant organization is only achieved by being politically correct. My true feelings and the tenets I believe in had to be suppressed in order to attain the status of where I now stand. I am disappointed with myself that I rationalized values to gain 'the day' and my position. It bothered me before I ever laid eyes on you. I was questioning what I was involved in. Michael, my answer is that I want to help! I want to make a difference. I want to be with you as a partner in making a better world!"

The rest of the night was planning. She gave Michael as much information about the complex as possible. It threw a totally different light on the operation. Michael now had some concrete facts that would allow them to make a plan based on actual conditions. He had been up all night, draining Doria of every bit of information. He slept soundly.

On the flight to London, Michael spent the time getting ready for Aron and Joshua. He had a feeling they knew about Doria and he now had the ammunition to lay out a positive plan. Before her information became available, they were just guessing. Now they could move with confidence and a working knowledge of the objective. Michael finally closed his eyes.

CHAPTER TWENTY

ARON AND JOSHUA FOLLOWED MICHAEL FROM THE AIR-
port. They did not see any surveillance of any kind. Michael went
straight to his apartment. They watched him enter. Again, nothing
out of the ordinary. They didn't want to wait until morning. It was
time to talk now. Michael knew by their presence they were aware
of Doria. They would have let him sleep if they were not concerned.
He seized the offensive before the questions started.

"Gentlemen, let me fill you in on the events since we last met."
He explained his relationship with Doria and how they had fallen
in love. He told them of his initial conversation in Sharm El Sheikh
and that this love affair was not a passing fancy but a genuine relationship that developed rather suddenly without warning. He told
them of his miscue of speaking in his sleep and Doria's realization
that something was not right.

"She could have put an end to me and the project by speaking to
Hassan. She said nothing. Everything came out last night when we
met at my apartment in Cairo. It was something I had never experienced. We both poured out our stories and I told her why I was there
and what the objective is. She told me about her life and what she
wants to accomplish. Doria is diametrically opposed to the projects
of Hassan and Nasser's plan for Egypt. She not only offered to help
but wants to play any role she can in bringing down both men and

their organizations. I don't have to tell you. You probably realized we were having a difficult time putting together the game plan we all signed off on. It was not going well. We were guessing, and that spelled failure if we could not find a better way. Doria has given us the path to achieving our goals. I brought this plan with me for your advice, your impressions, and your blessing."

They all looked at each other, trying to digest what was said.

Joshua stared at him. "That was a mouthful! You talked for an hour without us saying a word. Do we have the floor now?"

Aron lit his pipe and said, "We will get to the plan you brought shortly, but before that, can we ask you a few questions?

Question 1: Is all of this a figment of your imagination? We are not in the business of fairy tales.

Question 2: I know you are a hopeless romantic, but don't you think there's a possibility that Doria is setting you up?

Question 3: You are about to ask us to put our total trust in someone who is 'lovesick' and just made a deal with someone we would classify as the enemy?"

Aron paused and then continued speaking. "Tell me, I know at times we are risk takers with huge upsides and downsides. That's our business. We try to limit these swings and put a plan on the table that limits the extremes. Can you safely say we are in this realm? Don't answer. I want to hear the rest. I just want you to weigh your thoughts as you tell us about this miracle 'plan' that has fallen into our hands."

Michael nodded. "This is not going to be easy. You have two suspicious Israeli spies viewing a plan put forth by two lovebirds, one of whom apparently works for the enemy at the moment. Adding to that, one or both have zero experience in anything remotely similar to what is being proposed."

Joshua and Aron smiled, trying to hold back their reaction.

Michael continued his train of thought. "I was able to piece together a plan before I became involved with Doria. It was a plan in process that needed to be 'researched' with an exploratory, clandestine trip into the area of the warehouse and research facilities to finalize how to proceed. That's not needed today if we believe and follow the information given to us by Doria. Her knowledge and accessibility to both facilities throws my original plan out the window. She has given me a detailed picture, actually a map of the structures, their numbers and exact locations. More importantly, we know how to penetrate this area easily. Well, at least a lot simpler than how we would have approached the problem.

"It is now a trust issue. How can I convince you that working with Doria is not only our best option, it really is our only one? I made the decision to involve her, and she made the decision to join us. I am willing to put my life on the line, but I know that's not worth its weight if things go wrong and we have an international incident and a victory for Hassan and Nasser. I know the decision rests with you and your superiors. Can I tell you more about the problem before we discuss the actual plan?

"We are probably in the best position today than we've ever been since I arrived in Cairo. Hassan was suspicious of the project from the beginning and kept security details on our movements. We have finally sold him on our commitment to developing the business. As you know, he searched my apartment and used a security company to check my movements in London. What I learned from Doria is that he finally believes we are genuine and we have his total confidence. This is the time to move against him!"

Joshua emptied his pipe in the sink. "Michael, we will hear your plan in the morning. I believe you are right. It is the most viable route to achieve our goals. That is not the issue. We need to trust you and your analysis of the situation. There are always surprises in any plan. We both know that the best plans are not etched in stone. I have to speak with Tel Aviv and discuss all the ramifications. We will meet you at Fantastique to maintain your cover, just in case. Tomorrow morning at nine. Rest well and don't talk in your sleep!"

Michael did dream. It was a jumble of Doria, Hassan, and the plan. He woke up in a sweat and felt around in the dark for his watch. It slipped to the floor and he fell back to sleep.

Dawn came quickly and Michael was up, standing in a cold shower until he felt totally refreshed. He was in the office early and saw that Sir Arthur was already there.

"What are you doing here? You are supposed to be building a store and opening a factory."

"I guess that will have to wait a few days until I return. I'm expecting my brothers any time. We have a few things to discuss."

"Don't tell me. I don't want to know. Good luck!"

The boys arrived, and they took over Sir Arthur's private conference room.

"Michael, you have created a lot of midnight conversations and significant telephone charges. There is another phone conversation that needs to be made before we get down to the business at hand. There is someone who wants to speak with you. We are placing the call now."

"Yes, Prime Minister, I am that person."

"I have been listening to our people relay the progress of the project. We seem to be in a situation where we find ourselves changing a course in midstream. That course is usually set by the officer at the scene. He is the only one who totally understands what is involved. That person seems to be you. Are you up to the task? Are you aware of the responsibility? We are with you every step of the way."

Michael hung up the phone. Was that really him? They got started.

CHAPTER TWENTY-ONE

DORIA HAD MADE HER DECISION, AND SHE KNEW HOW IT would affect her life and that of Michael. Her whole outlook was different, for now she had cast her lot with Michael. She didn't feel as if she was being a traitor. Her desire to rid Nasser's rockets and his Nazi thugs from Egypt was now her cause. Hassan's munitions were only fueling the fires of hate and pain throughout the world. She felt good that she had made her decision. Michael would be back in a few days, and she had to make sure everything was in order.

As she was reviewing her thoughts and contemplating the eventsof the past day, Michael was in London laying out the plan.

Michael used the blackboard to lay out a diagram of the facilities. He had worked with Doria that night using her knowledge of the complex to make a rudimentary drawing based on her recall.

"Gentlemen, as you can see, the complex is much larger than we anticipated when planning this mission. Their facilities are developed way beyond our initial intelligence. I'm not sure of the total breakdown between Hassan's munitions and Nasser's research. I have marked some structures with stars that we think are cooling devices on the roofs. I am not sure why they are there. Your people should be able to give us the answers. All this came from Doria. The security fences between the two facilities are detailed here. They are possibly an issue. Doria is working on finding the answers. We now must decide how to destroy this menace. The original plan could not work based on the size of the facility and this new information."

Michael used a large sketch pad from his office and spent time resketching in great detail what he had drawn on the blackboard. While he was working on the sketches, the Israelis were plotting their new approach. Aron and Joshua reviewed all the information.

"Michael, we need to go to a secure site, which is our embassy, and speak with our friends at the Company regarding this new information you have acquired. We are fortunate to happen to have some of our 'brothers' here for other reasons, which will help immensely. It's now twelve noon. Let us meet back here at 4:30 p.m. and see how we have progressed. We have tomorrow, but we want to use that time to review our decision."

Michael looked at his watch and thought it was just after seven in the morning in Boston. He could call Hannah and Abe and Sarah to find out what was happening. Most importantly, he wanted to put their minds at ease.

Hannah was overjoyed to hear from Michael. She asked him everything she could think of regarding his well-being but did not pry into his personal life. Again, he reiterated that he was traveling and it was difficult for him to call. He assured her that he was well and taking care of himself, answering all the motherly questions.

Michael called Abe and Sarah. He caught them at home before they left for the office. Their conversation with him was quite different.

"Michael, what the hell is going on with you? We realize you need the break, but this lack of communication with us is quite disturbing. In plain, unadulterated English, we don't like it. We are worried about you and were about to call our friends in Israel to find out what is going on. You are making your mother crazy. I hope you have already called her."

Abe continued the lecture, softening it as he went along.

"First of all, we are selfish. You have created a position with us. We are dependent on your creative and executive skills in operating a very significant segment of this organization. We want you back. When will this occur? Besides that, we want to see your lousy face and put up with all those ideas you are constantly putting on the table. You are always on our minds and in our hearts. So, Michael, when will we see you? Come home soon! We love you!"

Michael danced around the question and implied that he was a few weeks away from coming home. His thoughts turned to his life and where it was going. "Will it be with Doria and my world of family and friends in Boston?" He could not think of anything he wanted more. The phone rang. It was almost 4:30 p.m., and they had returned.

Aron and Joshua came back with two additional Israelis, Mordecai and Avril. Both of them were in London for other reasons, actually coming from Washington, DC, where they were holding a high-level meeting with the CIA. They were not on holiday. Both were experts in rocket technology and explosives, and each had a list of questions for Michael.

The conference room had its own bar and small kitchen. Michael realized he had not eaten and took a sandwich from the small refrigerator. He started giving them answers as he gulped down the chicken salad with a cold drink.

"I have not seen the entire complex. I am relaying what was told to me by a very reliable source. The drawing depicts that number of buildings. If all the structures are constructed as the one I saw, I believe they are poured concrete. They have metal garage-type doors, which I recall opened hydraulically."

They were working with their slide rulers and calculators. They had analyzed the drawing of the layout and discussed the problem between themselves. Michael presumed they were calculating how many explosives were needed to eliminate the problem.

"If only Doria was here, we would not be making value judgments," Michael thought. He was confident his drawing was a good replica of what actually existed. They were not guessing.

Aron got up and stretched, hoping to alleviate some of the tiredness.

"Michael, any additional information you can think of?"

"I gave you everything, but let's go over each point. You never know what can come out. As far as Hassan's warehouses are concerned, I believe they are all laid out in an identical manner, steel shelving set up to accommodate the thirty-foot ceilings. I gave you this information. Most of what's there should make a bonfire, fireworks like we've never seen. The scientific buildings are filled with highly flammable chemicals and fuels. There are No Smoking signs everywhere."

"Michael, when you enter Hassan's domain to get to your Fantastique project, do you have to go through security?"

"I do not have to go through security to enter the Fantastique section. But I do need to, to go through the general entrance."

"What type of security is involved?"

"There are metal detectors. We are body-searched and all our briefcases and suitcases are opened."

"Do you know how supplies such as food enter the facility?"

Michael thought about it and remarked, "There is another commercial entrance that handles deliveries from suppliers. There is a security team that checks the arriving merchandise. They also use metal detectors."

Avril posed a question: "If we delivered a package to your apartment in Cairo, could you find a way, with the help of Doria, to get it sent to the Fantastique product development center in the complex?"

"I believe that could be done."

Michael laid out the pieces of the plan.

"We want to proceed on that basis. Now, let's get down to how we want you to get this accomplished. When we were giving you your training, we touched on explosive devices. We now feel this is the road we must travel. Let's talk about plastic explosives.

"As you know, they are a soft and hand-moldable solid form of explosive material. They can be described as putty explosives. Plastic explosives are especially suited for explosive demolition. The common ones are Semtex and C-4. Let's talk about C-4. As I said, its texture is similar to modeling clay and it can be molded into any desired shape. C-4 is stable, and an explosion can only be initiated by the combination of extreme heat and shock wave from a detonator. By shaping it to your desired form, you can change the direction of the explosion. Just for your knowledge, we can thank the British for developing its present form during World War II. It is very stable and insensitive to most physical shocks. You can drop it. It will not explode when set on fire. A detonator is needed to set it off. We will give you more information and show you how to make it work before you leave tomorrow."

Avril yawned and gained his composure.

"As I said, it will be our job to get the material to your apartment. You need to find the best way to bring it into the compound. The explosives will be packaged in a manner that will make it easier for you to bring through security. We are working on how we will do this. You will know when you receive the package. We will now show you how they should be dispersed to gain the expected results. This material is best to destroy concrete and steel, which is the makeup of the structures. Naturally the stored munitions and chemicals will light up the sky. We have a bit of luck in your favor, as Bengy is close to being an expert on C-4 and will solve any problems that arise. With Doria's information, he should be able to handle any issues. That sums up how we feel we should proceed. The ball is now in your court."

They ordered dinner in, for they wanted to cover as much ground as possible today. Michael wanted to return as quickly as possible. Getting this over with was his top priority.

Doria went through the motions of overseeing EgyptCo. Her thoughts were in London and on what was about to happen. She didn't know how they were going to proceed and was getting nervous wondering what the plan was to destroy the complex. She had gone back to Michael's apartment to bring him some food for his return. She would have met him at the airport but didn't want to be conspicuous by spending too much time with him.

Doria was unaware she was seen leaving the apartment. Mr. Nasr, who had dinner with Hassan and Michael on their initial meeting, lived in the same neighborhood. He was coming home from a late dinner and saw her leaving the apartment. He did not know where she lived, but he would check in the morning and find out who was living in the apartment complex where he saw her. Nasr was head of the General Intelligence Directorate with the title of chief of intelligence. He knew that Michael was his neighbor.

Michael arrived in fairly good shape even though it was a whirlwind three days. He contacted Doria in the morning and arranged to go to the compound. Doria did not say much over the phone. She just told Michael that Bengy and Avrom were fine and waiting for him. He suggested they all meet at the Fantastique office to go over where they were on the development and getting the production process working. He said he needed to meet in Cairo to also check with the real estate organization looking for locations.

Before Michael left, he was told to expect a package at his Cairo residence within five days. If he did not receive it by the seventh day, the whole operation was in trouble and he should leave Egypt. When he originally left for Egypt, he was given a second identity if needed. That passport, papers, and money were sealed in the lining of his briefcase. It could only be discovered if his briefcase was torn apart. What he demanded from the Israelis was a way out for Doria. She was to receive a passport and papers. It would be an Iraqi passport. All she needed to do was insert a photo. She would be given a cover that would give her a new identity and the ability to escape with Michael. The passport would come with the C-4 material. Michael went over all the instructions before departing for Egypt.

"How are you going to deliver the C-4 to my apartment?"

Aron spoke up. "None of your business. You will know when it arrives."

When Bengy and Avrom arrived at the office, he had the boys look for any listening devices. He wanted to tell them about Doria and her part in the operation. He did not tell them about his personal relationship with her.

Doria arrived a half hour later, as Michael wanted. They were all brought up to date on how they were about to proceed. The boys were more than surprised when they were told about Doria. They immediately reacted with hugs and handshakes. They thanked her for working to help their cause and hers. She told them her story.

They did not get specific instructions on how the C-4 would be placed but a general idea, depending on the size of the facility. They went through the details again, trying to poke holes in their plans. Michael used the blackboard to illustrate what they needed to accomplish. It did not stay on there long. They were super-cautious about their security.

Michael summed it up. "So, my friends, those are the details. It is an ambitious plan. But like all plans, nothing is perfect. We will need to improvise if things don't go exactly as we have laid them out. I do not expect this to be our final plan. It would be naive for us not to find additional information that will poke a hole in this strategy. Let's call it a 'possible solution' to our problem. We should keep thinking about how we can improve the process."

The plan was dependent on positioning of the C-4. Again, this could only be achieved by getting into the compound and following the instructions for placement given by the Israelis. Doria had many of the answers. Although she was not authorized to enter this zone, she knew where the keys were kept and felt the best way to acquire them was by copying them from a clay impression. This could only be done by her, although it needed coordination from all of them to create a diversion. It had to be worked out as soon as possible. Time was of the essence, and the longer it took to put the plan to destroy the complex into action, the greater the chance they would be discovered.

The next morning, Mr. Nasr followed through on checking the addresses of both Doria and Michael. Just as he thought! Mr. Amin's apartment was where Doria exited. He felt that would be interesting information for Hassan. He picked up the phone.

"Hassan, how are you? How about lunch today? We need to go over a few things."

The three of them were now at the compound and started to work. Michael had brought back additional patterns for them to develop. The product-development process was serving its purpose. They could move through a sufficient amount of the complex. This would allow them to help Doria get the impressions of the keys.

CHAPTER TWENTY-TWO

HASSAN MET NASR IN CAIRO. HE HAD BUSINESS THERE, so it was not inconvenient for him. It was a traditional Egyptian restaurant, and they ordered simple meals.

Nasr went through some of the many stories that were abounding in the city and throughout the country. There were always rumors circulating. Nasr tried to explain the reasons why.

Hassan listened, trying to be patient. "Come to the point, Nasr. Why did you want to see me?"

He explained what he saw while on his way home and thought it was worth bringing to Hassan's attention. "It was the other night."

Hassan made a note of the date. He was totally surprised and deeply concerned. He had placed his trust with Doria, and this was something he did not expect. He wanted an explanation, and he wanted it quickly. He had doubts on the project early on but resolved them. The program with Fantastique had great potential and was a feather in his cap for the development of his business in Egypt.

When Hassan arrived at Doria's office, she could see that he was not himself.

"Doria, I have gotten some distressing news today."

"What is it?"

"Why were you at Mr. Amin's apartment the other night? What is your relationship with him?"

Doria was stunned but did not lose control. "Hassan, Mr. Amin was returning from London the following day and I wanted to make sure he had food in the refrigerator. Why do you think that I have a relationship with him?"

"Doesn't he have a maid?"

"No, since he moved into the compound during the week, there was no need for her services."

"I am still upset that you have taken personal interest in Mr. Amin. I understand that you want to be a gracious host and keep him happy, but there are limits, and we have reached them now. Do you understand me?"

"Yes, Hassan. I am in accord." He turned and walked out of her office.

Doria sat at her desk trembling. Had she given him sufficient reason to believe her? She thought so but was still unsure. There wasn't any question that she had created problems that should not have occurred. His attitude toward her was now different. Would this create serious responses, for that was difficult to read at the moment? Hassan would be more aware of what was happening around him. That was certain. Their movements, although not restricted, would be monitored. She was sure of that. It would be different. "I wonder if he will say anything to Michael. We have to move quickly; time is on their side, not ours." She believed Hassan would heighten security.

Hassan decided not to say anything about his conversation with Doria, but he asked Michael for an update on how the project was going. Michael showed him some prototypes that had been developed and gave him an in-depth report on how they were progressing. Hassan seemed agitated.

"So tell me, are we doing our part to make this work? Is Doria giving you the support you need?"

Michael sensed something was wrong. It was not the usual conversation with Hassan.

"She has done a great job giving us all the help we have requested. The issue here is training the people to be good operators and gain an experience level. Unfortunately, that does not happen overnight.

"I'm sure we are headed toward a successful business together. The big mistake is to rush into production. Mr. Bannister and Mr. Clark are working to train and coordinate the necessary staff. No one wants a false start. The first items we ship have to be perfect. The worst thing we can do is ship bad goods. We then will destroy our credibility."

"So you are happy with us?"

Michael smiled. "Could you do better? Of course, but so can we. I am optimistic that it will happen. Let's give it the time to develop."

Hassan was pleased with the conversation. Michael showed no reaction to his mentioning Doria. He wanted to see how everything developed.

Both Michael and Doria believed they had weathered the storm. However, it curtailed any meetings in Cairo unless they were accompanied by Bengy or Avrom at the Fantastique office. Everyone was on high alert.

Aron and Joshua now had to deliver the C-4 to Michael. They had a number of avenues available. What was most important was that Michael receive the merchandise as quickly as possible without any issues. They realized the real problem was finding the way to bring it into the compound. They were dependent on Doria to work out the plan.

The quickest route to Cairo was through London. The Company had a Sayan in the Cairo area who agreed to do a favor for his friends. As soon as it arrived in London, it was routed to the correct agent and then to its destination.

The package came from Heathrow via air freight, addressed to Michael as personal property and sent to his apartment in Cairo. The paperwork showed apparel and personal toiletries, HANDLE WITH CARE! It was marked PRIORITY.

Doria had connections at customs and was able to get a priority clearance put on the package. Hassan's company, EgyptCo, brought merchandise through customs on a regular basis. It was not opened since the customs officials were well taken care of.

The concierge at the apartments received the package and held it for Michael's return on the weekend. There were a number of priorities that had to be addressed: Number one, to get the impressions of the keys that would allow them access to the off-limits sections of the complex. Number two, to scout out the locations needed to place the C-4 throughout Hassan's munitions and chemical departments and Nasser's rocket-development area. They had their work cut out for them.

The keys to the entire complex were located in the security office. There were a number of offices located in the executive building. Doria's office was between accounting and finance and Hassan's executive suite. Michael's office, along with Bengy's and Avrom's, was down the hall at the end of the corridor. They needed to create some sort of diversion to allow Doria to enter the security office and make the impressions.

They talked among themselves on how this could be done. The plan was to have some cleaning solutions, which were used on fabric, spill in the office and cause a fire. Their excuse would be that they were testing a new cleaner's ability to work on the fabric without staining or harming it. The alarm set off by Michael and the technicians would draw the security people from their offices and allow Doria to enter. The problem was how to make the fire look authentic. It needed to create significant smoke and commotion without getting out of control.

Four days before the "incident," Doria made sure there were fire extinguishers in the hallway. They had a fire alarm system that should, in their estimation, "wake the dead."

The fire was started. The immediate world responded, except Hassan, who was out of the country. They specifically chose that day knowing he would be elsewhere. Doria went into action as soon as the security people bolted from their office. She had at least six minutes, probably longer. It took her less than three minutes to have them put into clay and in her satchel before exiting.

Naturally, the fire would be reported to Hassan, but it would be a positive explanation. Security could say that it was contained and put out in record time with no apparent damage. The three of them played their parts well and there wasn't any reason on the part of security to believe it could have been anything other than an accident. Doria also did her part. She knew which keys were needed. Otherwise, it would have meant taking too many impressions. Part one had gone smoothly, but the rest of the plan would not be as easy to achieve.

They decided they needed to have an exploratory trip, although entering the off-limits area would be, as Michael put it, "pushing their luck." It could not be avoided. Getting the maximum placement was top priority. They studied the drawing that Michael put together and listened to Doria's comments, as she was the only one who actually had seen some of Hassan's facilities.

They had work to do. Timing was the key factor. Security made rounds, walking the compound on a regular timetable. They had to be in and out between the rounds.

What made the planning difficult was not knowing the exact number of structures that needed to be destroyed. Doria was not that sure how many existed. The unknown factors were the research facilities for the rockets. Did the Germans work late? Were there dogs in the compound? Was the security schedule the same for Nasser's section as it was for the Hassan warehouses? Somehow, they had to get these answers.

It was left to Bengy and Avrom to see what information they could get from their German friends in the dining room or at chess or exercise. They couldn't go forward without some or all of these questions resolved. In the meantime, they needed to develop a product and a production line. The charade had to go on.

CHAPTER TWENTY-THREE

THERE WAS ANOTHER PHASE OF THE OPERATION BEING developed far from Egypt. Even though there was an embargo on all materials that were considered munitions, chemicals, or related to rocketry, Hassan had found a way to circumvent these edicts. They were coming from Hassan's company, Nitcom, a Swiss/German firm. They employed many of the scientists who worked on the development of the V-2 rocket. Even though the West German government was policing the shipment of munitions, they could not stop the flow. Aron and Joshua wanted to stop the production of these weapons of mass destruction being shipped not only to Egypt but to the rest of the world. They had formed an alliance with the CIA and the UK M15 to put a stop to this production of weaponry. It was left to the Israelis to bring this problem to closure. The combination of illegal production at Hassan's plant and the destruction of his inventory in Egypt was the solution to the problem.

Nasser's rocket program could not function without Hassan's German/Swiss involvement. Hassan was more German than Egyptian. Having been raised in Europe and schooled in Germany and Switzerland, he had all the characteristics of his Prussian father and the same fervor as the ex-Nazis in their hatred of Israel. Hassan believed in Pan-Arab nationalism and supported Nasser and the Grand Mufti. He could not understand why the Egyptians, who outmanned the Israelis in every way, had failed. He felt it had to do with overconfidence; noncoordination with Syria, Jordan, and Iraq; graft; and poor judgement and planning. The rocket program would be put into effect and would negate the army's deficiency. The German involvement would bring consistency and the technology for success.

A bombardment of rockets on Tel Aviv would bring Israel to its knees. Hassan was sold on the strategy. His financing and development of the rocket program would be the key element for success. Hassan felt, under his leadership, he could harness the necessary pieces of technology and development to make the destruction of Israel a fact. The consensus among the US, UK, and Israel was simply that Hassan could not be tolerated. He was the maestro, and the orchestra could not play without him. What was needed was the total elimination of both. It fell to Aron and Joshua to make it a reality.

They had their hands full trying to destroy the German complex. Hassan had to die in an accident. He could not be assassinated. It could possibly happen in an explosion at his plant or in an auto accident. It would be fitting, as Michael's father had died in that manner. The problem was complex. Not the CIA, M15, or Israelis wanted to incur the wrath of the West German Republic. Although the West Germans wanted Hassan out of business, they could not stop him from exporting or developing products that were not included in the ban. His munitions and chemicals were being developed in an underground facility connected to the factory complex. Without Hassan's procurement of the necessary components, Nasser's rocket program would not exist.

Whatever was decided upon would go into action almost simultaneously with the explosions in his facilities in Egypt. They wanted the world to know this type of destructive power against all mankind would not be tolerated.

Their whole plan of attack was based on getting the explosives into the underground plant's ventilation system and setting off the flammable materials that were throughout the facility. One could easily believe a fire or an explosion was caused internally based on the materials being used for production. They did not want to have a high death toll. The event would be staged during off-work hours, caused by a malfunctioning machine generating sparks, a "dropped cigarette," or an electrical failure. The explanations were not difficult to understand.

Hassan was a different story. It would not be possible to have him in the vicinity of the accidental explosion. His demise would have to be thought out and carried out by a team put in place.

They devised a plan to learn his everyday schedule. Hassan would generally stay in Germany for two- to three-week periods. He did have security at his estate and a bodyguard driver for his armored sedan. He was divorced and visited his children weekly. Doria was right. He was homosexual but did not flaunt it. There were lovers throughout the years, but all of his affairs were very discreet. His current lover was a young scientist who worked for Hassan. They had met in Berlin and started seeing each other on a regular basis. Hassan was vulnerable, and they intended to take advantage of the situation.

On the weekend, Michael returned to Cairo to retrieve the parcel that had arrived. He had spoken with the concierge, who informed him he was holding a package that had arrived from his company. The concierge had a key to Michael's apartment, and Michael asked him to leave the package there. Michael brought the package to his office and met with all. It was now Doria's job to bring the C-4 into the complex without problems. Her plan was simple. Fantastique should have sent the package directly to Michael by way of EgyptCo. It had already gone through customs and EgyptCo's control at the airport. It had never been opened. Doria personally took it through security. It went through without any search.

Bengy and Avrom were now trying to gather as much information from the Germans as they could. They were now friends, dining together and kicking a soccer ball around in the exercise yard. They played chess almost every evening, and there was small talk. It was quite interesting to see how much intelligence they were able to uncover "accidently on purpose." Bengy spoke German, which was quite an advantage. He manipulated the conversation around areas of information that were vital.

Bengy started the conversation. "I see that you are cool and not sweaty. You come to dinner without taking a shower. We are sweating away on the production line."

Alex moved his bishop. "Oh, we have air-conditioning where I work. The temperature and chemicals must be controlled. We have two sections dedicated for research, where it is absolutely necessary to keep the chemicals from overheating. Otherwise, we would be sweating like you."

Bengy countered, moving his queen. "We have a warehouse and a new production line along with the old lines that were making sheets. How large is your section?"

"Oh, I believe it's four sections, including warehousing."

Bengy took his castle.

"We are only working days, even though we are behind schedule. Do any of you work nights?" There was a definite "Nein."

The pieces were falling into place. Systematically, they were able to put a picture together of what they could expect. They were reaching a point where they had to decide on the timing of the "expedition" into enemy territory. Doria came into Michael's office in the factory. She was smirking and in good humor.

"President Nasser has invited you to be his guest at a state dinner this coming week. You will now have the opportunity to meet our president and mingle with the ruling party executives. Hassan and I have also been invited. I'm not sure whether he will return in time to be there. There will be a whole contingent of Nazi scientists and technicians, so you will meet some firsthand. I will be your 'date' and act as your guide. Nasser seems to be interested in our project. He feels that an apparel industry will create work, especially for women. It will be black tie, so we will need to get you fitted for a tuxedo, unless you brought one."

He laughed. "I can get one in Cairo."

"You will be seated close to Nasser, so be prepared to answer questions. In one way, I am glad you're meeting him, and in another way, I am not. Nasser will surely do a check on you after the dinner."

Michael had spent time studying Nasser's rise to power. It was an important part of his "education" by Aron and Joshua. He was feeling that adrenaline rush as he entered the hall for the festivities. Meeting Nasser was proving to be more of a test than he anticipated. He didn't have time to think about it as Abdul Nasser appeared before him.

"Well, Mr. Amin, I am happy to make your acquaintance. Hassan and Doria said nice things about you even though you're British with an American accent." They laughed.

"I am very much interested in this project you are working on with EgyptCo. It could mean significant employment for our people. I am a champion of women's rights, and giving them an opportunity to work is a major step forward." Michael thanked him.

"I would hope that this plant will be one of many that will be part of the economic growth of Egypt. I want you to sit near me, as I have many questions." They continued the conversation in Arabic.

And so the evening passed by. Michael was asked about everything related to apparel and also about the political climate in the UK. It seemed both of them never stopped talking.

At first, Doria was concerned, but Michael was more than holding his own. He began asking Nasser about the difficulties in the Middle East. You could see that Nasser liked him, as he would never have engaged him if he didn't.

"You are quite astute. Your thinking is interesting."

"So tell me, Daniel, what do you think of our situation with the Israelis?" Michael didn't expect that question.

"Mr. President, I am in the apparel business. My horizons are to build our business where and however it can be done profitably. It might one day take us to Israel. We are an international company. Markets open and close. We must be aware of what can happen. There is always a major investment of time and money entering a country or leaving. We are experiencing this here with you. In fact, this is a major undertaking, as we want not only to develop retail but also a manufacturing base for our international business. We must have stability if we enter any market around the world. So my question is: are we in a positive situation here in Egypt?"

Nasser looked at him and smiled. "I can see why your company sent you. You seem to understand us. At least that's my first impression. I hope it's a lasting one. You will go far, young man."

The evening was a success. He had an opportunity to dance with the president's wife, who was extremely charming. He had one dance with Doria, who was elated with his handling of the president. They said very little to one another. One never knew who was listening.

To their surprise, Hassan arrived almost at the end of the dinner. He had just landed from Germany. Nasser greeted him warmly. You could see they had more than just a business relationship.

"You have a gem here, Hassan. I've been speaking with him all evening. He is a doer, and that's exactly what both of us need. I hope you are giving him all the cooperation he and his company need. He is also not afraid to speak with me, which I like. I want to see more of him."

Hassan looked at Michael. "You seem to have gained his confidence. I compliment you."

Doria sat next to Hassan. "I was under the impression that you were staying in Germany longer."

"Something important came up. I will only be here less than a week and then return. How is everything going? I heard about the fire. Is everything back to normal?"

"It was just an accident. I think the flames were extinguished in a few minutes at the most. Thank God there were fire extinguishers along the hall. I have to say, the security people did their job."

"How is the project going? Our friend Nasser has taken an interest, which means he will want to see results. Mr. Amin is now the center of attention, which means he must perform. Our leader would not appreciate all that talk ending in failure. I need to talk with Nasser. That's why I returned. Are you behaving?"

Doria looked at him. "Do you think I am not?"

"I have no doubt our little talk put you back on track."

"I was never off the track. Sometimes being a good Samaritan is taken the wrong way."

Hassan got the last word. "We want to make sure Mr. Amin is focused on the project. Enough said."

Chapter Twenty-Four

ARON AND JOSHUA WERE SLIGHTLY CAUGHT OFF GUARD. They anticipated Hassan being in Germany for a longer period. They wanted to coordinate their efforts with Egypt. The Company wanted all of this to happen within the same time period. It was necessary to find out when Hassan would be returning.

Everyone agreed it would be better to wait on the "scouting trip" until Hassan returned to Germany. If anything went wrong, they would have a better chance of escaping the complex. Up until now it was all theory, planning, reconnaissance, and conversations. They now realized they were on the firing line. There was a distinct possibility of failure, resulting in being discovered. There is always fear of the unknown, and Michael was no different from any other mortal. He knew this would not be a walk in the park and failure would cause liabilities, not only personally but to many.

The Company's unwritten law was "do not get caught," which Michael had engrained in his head. Self-preservation now had an additional aspect. It was called Doria. No matter what, they were both in this together.

Doria told Michael of Hassan's conversation. "It must have been extremely important for Hassan to return just to have a meeting with Nasser. He will only be here a few days and return. Something is in the wind."

Michael responded without hesitation.

"Let's see if Hassan gives us any clues. Maybe the Germans will know something more. It must relate to the rocket program. In the meantime, we need to find out as much information as possible about the research facility. I will have a conversation with Bengy and Avrom if Hassan's meeting with Nasser brings about any changes or events with the research section.

Doria brought out another aspect of the conversation.

"Hassan was not overjoyed with your being in such good graces with Nasser. If this project is successful, Hassan wants to take full credit. He now has to share it with you. That also means failure."

Hassan could not wait to see Nasser and tell him of his findings. He actually called for an appointment. There was a considerable amount of ground to cover, and he wanted his undivided attention.

He had met earlier in the day with the senior scientist working on the project. The information he was bringing had a direct bearing on how they would proceed. Dr. Deichman had worked on the V-2 project in the Reich and was an important contributor to the project. With the help of the Odessa, he had made his way to Argentina. When Nasser "invited" German scientists to join the ranks of ex-Nazis to work on a similar project, Deichman did not hesitate and came to Egypt. He achieved asylum and riches and wanted to work for the destruction of Israel.

Hassan laid out the program. "My friend, I bring excellent news. We have now achieved our goal, a V-2 rocket that will fly. They are ready to be sent to you."

His meeting with Deichman covered the new breakthrough. A rocket ready to fly within a month was greeted with applause. The issue was developing the launcher and final testing. That was the doctor's specialty.

Deichman was excited. "Deliver me the missile, and I will make it fly to Tel Aviv."

Hassan was impressed. He spoke of the issues.

"The problem will be getting it here. We are under around-the-clock surveillance by the West German government and, without a doubt, by the Israelis. It must be done, and I will need major help from Nasser to get it here. That is why I came to Egypt."

Hassan's meeting with Nasser was on schedule.

Nasser was in good spirits. "So, my friend, you didn't make the trip just to attend my dinner? Why are you here?"

Hassan reiterated the story he told Deichman and filled him in on some related issues.

"Tell me, Hassan, how do you assess the Israeli situation? Do you feel you have it under control? Have they penetrated your organization?"

"I feel the Israelis always have some sort of a presence around my organization. I don't have any one thing to substantiate my feelings, but I sense they are very real. They are tightening the noose around my neck worldwide. It is much harder for me to do business. I believe they have the Americans, the British and, naturally, the Germans putting pressure on my organization. Do you sense anything going on here in Egypt? Do you have any information from your security forces about any operations that could be under way?"

Nasser pondered his words for a moment.

"Hassan, I cannot guarantee they are not here. I do not feel they have made any serious inroads with their agenda. If you are right with your timetable and can deliver the rockets and we can develop the launch system, it is really not relevant. In my estimation, they are here, but they are not organized or ready to make a move against us. If you can deliver these components, we will strike first and it will be a death blow. So let's go about this properly. We have the advantage."

Nasser reiterated his thoughts. "I do not want a disaster, a missile gone astray or explosion in our complex. So we need to push the program forward but based on good judgment."

They talked about finances. Hassan's munition deliveries were being hampered by the group they discussed. This created some cash-flow problems, as he needed funds and now Nasser was his major source.

There was discussion on the political situation in West Germany and the many factors Nasser was facing at home and in the Middle East. Arab unity was only superficial. The chasm between Sunni and Shiite was deep and only served Nasser's enemies.

Hassan had to deliver the missiles, and the German scientists had to develop the launching system. Success for both Hassan and Nasser hinged on achieving that goal. The plan was to be ready in one month. It was a very ambitious program, but most of the pieces were already in place. It could work.

Michael sent word through Fantastique to Aron and Joshua that Hassan was here for a short time and had major talks with Nasser. The telex went straight to Sir Arthur, who called someone in London immediately. It was sent to the Israeli embassy.

Herr Deichman sprang into action using all his resources to work on the launching system. He gave his group a highly motivational speech ensuring them that with a successful launch, they would strike a mortal blow to the Jews.

Hassan did not tell Herr Deichman that this new missile could be fitted with radioactive cobalt. This was his secret. In fact, even Nasser was unaware of the lethal power about to be released. He wasn't sure Nasser would go along with this weapon. He would tell him in good time.

Bengy and Avrom did not have to wait long to pick up valuable information. They were now "pals" and on a first-name basis with the Germans. Steiger and Hirsch loved to gossip. Their social scene was limited, and the Israelis offered them an opportunity to use their social skills. Bengy played the perfect role as the anti-Semitic Englishman showing no love lost for the Jews or Israel. He played up the fact that some of his friends were killed by the Haganah before the British left Palestine and the State of Israel was created. He got all the news daily from them. Needless to say, what they heard shocked them and brought a whole sense of urgency to the operation.

Michael wanted to get this information to Aron and Joshua. He decided he would send Avrom to London. The excuse would be some acute allergies that were causing problems. This message had to be delivered in person. There was too much at stake.

There was an additional major point the Company needed to know. A change in plan was key, for there wasn't time for an exploratory trip. With the events that had transpired, time was becoming a major factor.

Michael wanted to know what would be the outcome of this new information. Could they stop the missiles from coming to Egypt? If they couldn't, there would be added pressure and incentive to destroy the facilities. It was imperative they have the information. He was not concerned there were now only three of them. They could get the job done now that Doria had supplied the missing elements. Naturally, the key was stopping the missiles before they left Germany or Europe.

The telex read that Avrom would be coming back to London immediately for serious health reasons. This was a clear signal he had to be met and debriefed. The message was received and acted upon.

Within hours of landing in London, Avrom met with Aron and Joshua. The news caused silence and deliberation from all. They had flown to London from Germany and met at his hotel. Michael's change in plan was understood. It put more pressure on all involved but could not be avoided. They were totally surprised hearing of the progress Hassan had made with the rocket program. Their information turned out to be way out of date. That was a major concern, and they wanted to get to the bottom of it. Somehow, they were off track, and without the news coming from Michael's team, they would be at a terrible disadvantage.

Doria, Michael, and Bengy had spent hours going over the strategy to place the C-4. They now had to finalize their departure from the complex once it was destroyed. There would be utter chaos once the structures were ablaze. If they placed the explosives without being discovered, their departure from the complex would not be an issue. After some thought, they all realized this was not realistic. Their only hope for a clear getaway was with the unknown contact. The escape plan was not in their hands. They would have to activate him shortly, for there were too many questions that only this person could answer.

Michael thought the person must be someone in Hassan's organization who already knew who they were. The more he thought about the plan, the more he realized the escape hinged on the contact. If that failed, they were in the hands of Doria, who wanted them to make their way to Alexandria. He let Doria speak but knew better. He had faith in Tel Aviv, for the contact would bring them to safety. Each of them now had a new identity. Michael and Bengy had them in the lining of their suitcases. Doria's had come with the C-4.

Hassan was getting ready to leave in the next few days and wanted to be updated on the progress of the joint venture. They had a meeting the following day, and Michael took him step-by-step through the product-development cycle, explaining each step. Bengy gave him a quick synopsis of how the workforce was being developed. Hassan wanted the information, as he felt Nasser would ask him at their final meeting before his departure. He asked numerous questions, all of which were answered with clear, positive, well-structured statements. He seemed to be pleased.

"I hope what you have so well described will turn into reality. It seems you are on the right track. We now have Nasser on our backs . . . no excuses."

Tel Aviv was assessing all the information from Avrom, Michael, Aron, and Joshua. They also had a report from their man in Cairo. The news about Hassan's breakthrough was extremely unsettling and demanded a reaction.

There was a plan in effect, led by Aron and Joshua, to destroy the facility in Essen. The question was: was the rocket still in the research facility, or had it been moved? No one knew categorically one way or the other. The research center had to be destroyed with the distribution center. Could it all be taken care of with one act? Was it possible to arrive at a definitive answer?

After a follow-up meeting with Nasser, which centered on finance, Hassan returned to Germany. He stopped in Zurich to check on the funds that were coming from Nasser and his Middle Eastern allies.

He felt more secure when all that was promised was in place. Once in Germany, his main objective was to move the two rockets to Egypt. He made the right decision moving them out of the research center. Hassan was certain the facility had been compromised, not only by the West Germans but also by the Israelis. He had found a clever way to move them. Hassan's company had what they called a "carnival day" every summer. They brought in a carnival company with rides and shows for the staff and families. The two rockets were camouflaged as part of the carnival, leaving the facility. They were now in a rented warehouse awaiting shipment to Egypt. The last stage of moving them to Cairo was not an easy task.

There were several itineraries that seemed feasible. He could have them trucked to a number of ports on the Mediterranean, where he had influence. They could be sent by air, trucked to a friendly airport, and on to Cairo. They ruled out Germany and France, as the customs and internal security were difficult and had been alerted. It could be Istanbul or Athens or even Belgrade. There was more than one option.

His right-hand man, Herr Schmidt, had researched every conceivable route and option. They even considered dismantling the device and sending it through numerous and diverse routes. It wouldn't work. The feasibility to get it right was too complicated. In the end, they needed a plan that would avoid detection by the Jews and the forces against them. They had found the way to bring the missiles out of the factory. The journey to Egypt was now possible. Hassan did not want any slip-ups and was personally in charge of planning and confirming the route.

When Aron and Joshua confirmed the missiles were no longer at the facility, they sprang into action, bringing additional agents to search.

There was now an eight-person team from Tel Aviv in Germany. The hunt for the missiles was top priority. Aron and Joshua headed up the team and concentrated their efforts on searching the immediate area, believing they were stored in the vicinity of the research center. They concluded that Hassan would not let them out of his sight, at least his immediate sight. They would have him under twenty-four-hour surveillance, hoping he would lead them to the rockets. They had a totally different set of problems now that the missiles were out of the research center.

The original plan was to destroy everything, thinking all was under one roof. Now, that could not be achieved. The missiles were priority, and for now, all the effort was centered on solving this problem. Aron and Joshua were convinced Hassan would move them by air. He did not have the patience for a sea voyage and their being out of his control for a longer period of time. They knew all the options and set their plan in motion.

Hassan decided on Rome. It was a short flight to Cairo, and he felt he had enough connections at Fiumicino to circumvent any issues. They would be trucked to Italy with all the necessary paperwork. What worked at the complex could work again there. He would pack the rockets between carnival machinery that was being shipped to Egypt. Hassan had the option at the last minute just to send the rockets disguised as machine parts.

Tel Aviv was using all its influence at every airport on their list to check every manifest to Egypt. It was a massive undertaking with too many opportunities to avoid detection. They assumed Hassan would use Rome, Athens, or Belgrade. They also ruled out any shipments that involved a change of planes. Most likely, it would be a nonstop flight to Cairo or Alexandria.

Aron went to Rome and Joshua went to Athens. Belgrade was eventually ruled out. It was highly unlikely they would use London or Paris. They had somewhat of an advantage, for they had Sayanim at both airports. These people, although not Israelis, wanted to help in any way, and the information they put forth was invaluable. They checked trucking invoices and all manifests to these key locations.

Hassan could not leave the project in the hands of others. He needed to be at the scene and see the merchandise off. His staff arranged a private plane so he could have the flexibility to make a decision at the last minute. That was his strategy, feigning movement here and going in a different direction at the last moment. Hassan had to file a flight plan, which was picked up by Israeli agents.

The search was centered on Rome. What failed to show up was an additional flight plan for the following day.

Hassan had some decisions to make. Should he divide the rockets and send them separately from two locations, or should he gamble and go from one? His plan, naturally, was to create some type of diversion. He needed to truck the rockets to their departure point for shipment.

Hassan acquired two additional carnival trucks so he could send each to Rome, Athens, and Belgrade. There would be three shipments to Cairo from separate ports. Only one would carry the rockets. They were sent to Athens, where the overall systems were lax and customs officials were known to turn a blind eye. Even though Joshua was there, no one could control or check all the shipments.

Hassan's flight plan to Rome triggered total emphasis on the part of the Israelis. By the time they seized the Rome shipment, Hassan had flown off to Athens and seen his shipment off to Cairo.

What could they say? They had been outmaneuvered by a professional. The problem of the destruction of the missiles or V-2 rockets now fell on Michael's shoulders. There was another plan that Tel Aviv really didn't want to carry out unless they were forced to do so.

Tel Aviv was limited in what it could do for Michael. He had the explosives and a plan to destroy the facilities. Was it too much to ask? With the rockets now in Nasser's hands, the level of difficulty was considerably higher. Security around the weapons would be heightened. Was their plan sufficient to overcome a completely different situation?

Chapter Twenty-Five

Somehow or another, they had to create a plan that would bring about the destruction of the rockets, research facility, and munitions. The threesome went over the layout of the compound to see if they could come up with a solution that would bring total chaos throughout the facility. Creating this scenario would allow them to maneuver at will.

Bengy was more of an engineer than Michael. He was sort of a mathematician involved in a new idea of communication his Israeli comrades were working on. He had come up with a whole new approach to the plan and wanted to run it by them.

"There are five water towers adjacent to the executive offices, research facilities, and warehouses. There could be additional ones, but that seems to be the total. They hold tons of water, and if we create explosions or have them let go in a series, this could be our ticket to success and escape. If we place the charges 'creatively,' the explosions will bring about a 'biblical flood.'"

The question was how to release the waters at the right time. They did not want to be washed away.

"I need to do some math and possibly some physics to see if it will work and keep us from drowning or being blown up."

The Germans were quick to tell Bengy of the coup as he allowed them to win at chess. The rockets were here and they were housed in the research section so they could be fitted to the launching system.

Hassan returned to Germany from Athens, contented the missiles were in the hands of Nasser. He felt a sense of accomplishment, for his major task now was to get his international arms sales in full gear. He would soon not have to be concerned with the Israelis.

Nasser would be the "ultimate hero" of the Arab world. His triumph would bring him the Pan-Arab nationalistic state that was his dream. Jordan, Syria, Iraq, Yemen, and the new State of Palestine would be his domain. Hassan wondered if he could possibly be controlled. It was not a problem for today. He wondered how his English partners were doing as he sent a telex to Doria.

Aron and Joshua licked their wounds and focused their attention on destroying Hassan's German facilities. They put into action the plan they had formulated. It centered around the subterranean development center that had developed the rocketry. They wanted Hassan to be part of the explosion if it could be arranged. It was now a very personal issue, for their defeat by his hands was difficult to swallow. They would use the ventilation system for the underground facility to place the explosives.

All three agreed it was time to activate Tel Aviv's person in Egypt. His or her help was going to be needed in every aspect of the operation. To reach the contact, Michael had to return to his apartment and put an empty envelope in his mailbox. He would be contacted within twenty-four hours.

The contact would approach Michael and ask him, "Do you intend to vacation on the Riviera?"

"I thought I would go to Cannes."

"Well, you should go to Juan Le Pen." That confirmed the authenticity.

Michael went back to the apartment, and as he got off the elevator and walked the dark corridor, he heard the phrase he was waiting for. Out of the shadows stepped Mr. Nasr. Michael could not believe who he was seeing. He was in shock, at least for the moment. They were in front of his apartment, and Michael fumbled with the key. Nasr took it away and opened the door.

"I know you are in shock. I'm probably the last person in the world you expected. Don't put on the lights until the shades are drawn."

"Why did you tell Hassan about Doria's visit here?"

"First of all, you were not here and it could be considered a harmless visit. I saw her on my way home. I was not alone. My driver is in the private security force of Nasser. I really didn't have any choice. I know you have a thousand questions as to how I got here, but let's put that aside and consider the problem."

They talked about a number of options, but Michael did not divulge what he thought could be the answer. He wanted to believe Nasr was their man. He needed time for it to sink in. He gained his composure.

"We need your help. We are formulating a plan. When everything is finalized, we would want your input. When can we meet again?"

"I was there at Sharm el Sheikh and saw your developing relationship with Doria. Tel Aviv requested I go."

Michael smiled. "If I had known that you were on our side, I would have had you run interference for us!"

Nasr was bewildered.

"Never mind; it's an American expression!"

Luckily, they had a meeting set up in Michael's Cairo office.

"You know, I feel much better about the entire situation. Nasr will be a major asset to us getting this done and, hopefully, getting us out of these circumstances. Now I want to hear from Bengy."

"I believe our best chance for success lies in using this whole concept of the water towers. So let me tell you how I think it can work. I am not an expert . . . far from it. Let me give you an explanation of how it can work.

"A water tower, as we know it, is an elevated structure supporting a water tank, constructed at a height sufficient to pressurize a water-supply system for distribution of potable water and to provide emergency storage for fire protection. That's what it's supposed to do. How does it work? They rely on hydrostatic pressure produced by the elevation of water due to gravity to push the water into domestic and industrial systems. As we can see, these water towers are made of reinforced concrete with steel. They are spherical. They reduce the need for electrical consumption, although I believe in this case they are just used for backup. These towers hold about eight thousand gallons, possibly more. The pressure or force of the water will do exactly what we need. How do we do this?"

Bengy used the blackboard as he spoke. He gave a full explanation, hitting every point.

"If we can set off the towers at the right intervals, it will be the determining factor for success. It will cause such chaos that we will be able to enter the restricted area and place the C-4. The water released will flood the security offices, all the sleeping quarters for the entire complex, the executive offices, and the Fantastique product-development center and factory. That section of the compound will be out of action. It will 'freeze' the security detail. There will be little opposition, probably none, if the timing is right.

"Timing? It should be done, naturally, at night, probably two to three in the morning. It will catch everyone totally off guard and confused, sending torrents of water upon them. The sound of the water itself will create panic. I cannot believe otherwise. Whether it is three or four of us working quickly, we should be able to detonate the entire complex.

"Any security people or workers in the warehouse will be totally frightened by the noise and the water. It should create a scene of total confusion, for they will be running to safety. We should be free to move. In regard to setting the charges, it should not be difficult to achieve maximum destruction, as we are dealing with munitions and chemicals, all extremely combustible. Our major objective is the rockets. If nothing else happens, we will have done the job.

"I believe there needs to be a delay between the two explosions or, should I say, the initial water tower detonations and the explosions of the facilities. As I said, timing is crucial. This needs some real thought. Nasr could be immensely helpful with this problem. I would like to consult with him.

"The water towers are all located outside the restricted area, and most are adjacent to exactly where we need them. The balance is in front of the warehouses and research facility. There is a question as to when we should release these towers, before or possibly after the explosions are in process. The timing is crucial. I need time to figure things out.

"My thoughts at the moment are they should be used to cover our escape. We need to do some additional planning. Let's see if the strategy holds up to our questions and ideas. What I think we should do is get started as soon as possible setting the C-4 on the towers. They are outside the wire and can be approached without major difficulty."

Michael got up and hugged him. "You are our in-house genius! We are in your hands."

Michael agreed and wanted to get together with Nasr to discuss all the issues. Bengy wanted to hear Nasr's thoughts on his plans for the escape.

Nsar proceeded in a very deliberate tone. "I have several ideas that can be put into place. It depends on what we decide to do. The major plan on the table is putting you in a safe house in Cairo and using your second identities to move you out of Egypt the best possible way. I cannot be more specific at the moment about the route. It depends on so many factors. I believe the safe house is the only plan right now that makes sense. I will get all of you there safely. I would like to maintain my position and not be exposed so I can continue to do my work. Naturally, it would be best if I can get you out of the country quickly. I think it would be a mistake to push for immediate travel plans. When should we move forward?"

Michael said, "As we discussed, I would like to get this done while Hassan is not here. His presence will only create serious problems for all concerned. Doria, do you know his schedule?"

"I believe he will be in Germany for another ten days to two weeks."

"His schedule will set our game plan. I would like to ask if Nasser has any plans to come here."

Nasr came directly to the point. "Not to my knowledge. When this occurs, he will be on the warpath. No one likes to be made a fool, so expect a full-scale search for us. All the avenues out of the country will be sealed. We will have to be at our very best to find a way out. If we can leave the compound as we are planning and I can maintain my cover, we will be in a position to know his moves. I plan to be disguised and use a stolen car for our departure."

Michael paused and then said, "So let us set a date. We need to notify our friends, and Nasr has to make final plans for the safe house."

"Bengy, how do you plan to get us out of here? How should we expect to flee the compound? How will Nasr be involved?"

Bengy went to the blackboard once more. "My thinking is as follows. There is a roadway around the water towers leading eventually to the highway. There are gates in the fence in front of every water tower that faces the warehouses and research center. When the charges are set, we can leave the complex through these gates. We have keys. Remember, the water tower will be roaring down on the security offices, sleeping quarters, etc., so we should have little opposition to leave the compound in this manner. The explosion will follow. When Nasr picks us up in the van on the roadway, the additional water towers will blow, creating another wave of panic and confusion, allowing us to get away. Our main concerns are the warehouses and the research center. Two of us will have to do double duty. Nasr will be in the car. That's roughly how it should work. We will get all the details straight. We have to go over the C-4, how it works, placement, and detonation. There's a lot to do and not a hell of a lot of time. Any questions?" They laughed.

Chapter Twenty-Six

Aron and Joshua now had the date Michael and team would go into action. They wanted to coordinate their plans accordingly. The ideal situation was to destroy the facility while Hassan was there. If he was not included in the explosion, they had made additional plans. Their choice of materials was the same as those being used in Egypt. They were counting on passing off the explosion as an accident, setting off the chemicals and explosive devices used in their experimentation. There would obviously be repercussions from the West German government. Actually, they would be relieved to know that Hassan and his factories were gone. When the public discovered it was a secret underground operation, public opinion as well as the government would condone the action.

Tel Aviv was extremely concerned about whether Michael's team could pull it off. "The Hammer" was the name Tel Aviv gave the plan. There was an alternative they would activate if Michael failed. The option was to send in low-flying aircraft under the radar that would decimate the facilities, killing everyone. Michael could be a casualty if he and his team could not get away. The mission had to be achieved no matter what. Michael was informed through Tel Aviv that if he was unable to execute his plan by a certain date, he should use Nasr's escape route.

The best-laid plans, as the saying goes, always somehow go astray. The chances of everything going like clockwork are generally a pipe-dream. It was hard to believe! Somehow the gods of Abraham or the gods of whomever were smiling upon them. The plan went off on time. The charges had been set days before on all the water towers. Bengy and Michael had done the work with blackened faces, sweat pouring through their dark fatigues. They were fortunate not to have run into any security, mainly because it was not a primary target for the security forces. All the towers were wired. They were ready to go.

Doria had made additional keys in case they were needed. When the first tower burst, cascading more than eight thousand gallons down on the sleeping and security facilities, they believed it would bring whoever was in the warehouses and research areas running to see what was happening. They would open the gates for the three-some to do their work. Just as Bengy outlined, when the roar of the water rocked the silence of the night, all hell broke loose, creating the expected reaction. There was total confusion, allowing Michael, Bengy, and Doria to enter the structures that needed to be destroyed. Michael entered the research center and placed the charges directly on the rockets. He was the only one who ran into some interference. One of the scientists had been working late and was screaming at Michael. There was so much noise and commotion that Michael could not hear what he was saying. Instead of conversation, he hit him across the face with a wrench he was carrying, knocking him out. All warehouses were done in record time with no casualties.

Bengy made sure Doria's portion was completed. She didn't really need the help, but he wanted to be certain she didn't run into any opposition. Their plan was to go to the gates to meet Nasr. All the charges were set. They wanted to be at a safe distance, for the explosions would be all-consuming and spectacular. They would be seen miles away, and the explosions would send shock waves quite a distance. They really didn't know how ferocious the explosions would be, as they were not bomb specialists.

They set the charges so they would go off in sequence. First, the research facility that made the rockets, followed by the warehouses, one after another. They knew if they went off all at once, it would also kill them. All three made their way to the road, where Nasr was waiting. He was dressed as an Arab, with beard and flowing robes.

It was hard to believe that they had gone through the drill, the real one, without a mishap. They stood there for a minute, not believing they had pulled it off.

"It actually worked!" were the words out of Bengy's mouth. As they pulled away, they could see the devastation caused by the water and the complete confusion.

The first charge went off, and it was a massive, incredible explosion, throwing debris into the air over a hundred-foot area. They kept looking as the warehouses started to explode. The earth shook. The shock waves almost caused the van to go off the road. It went on as if it was a fireworks display a hundred times over. The noise was deafening. The sky became a smoldering caldron of reds and oranges and blackened clouds. It could be seen all the way to Cairo.

When the explosions subsided and there were just the fires, the balance of the water towers would let go and flood the compound grounds. It was phenomenal. They could not believe the results. The world was on fire.

Nasr drove toward Cairo. He did not speed but kept going at a reasonable clip. They saw the fire brigades heading toward the complex. Doria looked through the rear window as the sky was ablaze.

All she could think of was what fury would be unleashed by Hassan and Nasser. They were fortunate to have done their work. She knew that the wrath of both of them would know no limit.

"They will never stop hunting us."

Michael could see the fear in her eyes. He knew what she was thinking, for similar thoughts were on his mind. Bengy was still basking in the great win. He was about to come down to earth shortly.

Nasr was pleading with them to keep themselves down. He had brought Arab outfits for all three so they would be able to exit the car when they arrived at the safe house. They were now quite a few miles from the complex, and at four in the morning, the sky had turned to orange. Everyone was up along the road not knowing what happened.

Both Michael and Doria knew the real ordeal was before them. He heard the words from his tutors—"Rule number one: Don't get caught! Rule number two: Don't get caught!" They were in the hands of Nasr, hoping he would get help from Tel Aviv. They were finally in Cairo. All three put on their Arab outfits. Nasr was now weaving his way through the labyrinth of streets to find the safe house. Michael's study of the city came into play. He knew where they were, for he had walked this area. The sun was just rising and the darkness was receding into the shadows. He was racing to get them situated as he had to be back to his post with the directorate. He only had a few hours before he should be startled by a call from his office about the calamity.

Hassan's German operation suffered the same fate. The underground research facility that developed the rockets was incinerated as Aron and Joshua had planned. The entire subterranean structure was completely demolished. His regular warehouse suffered almost the same fate, with very little left standing. The authorities were now involved, wanting to know what caused such a tremendous explosion in a facility that was not supposed to exist. There was a lot of explaining to do, but Hassan was nowhere to be found. As far as Aron and Joshua were concerned, the job was only half done. They had personal business with Hassan.

It took two days for Nasser to sort out what had occurred. He toured what was left of the compounds with his staff. He said nothing, for it was all on his face. All he could think of was finding these Israelis. The entire security forces would be used to find these terrorist Jews.

"Where was Hassan? How could he have been fooled? How could I be taken in by this Amin or whatever his name is?"

"Well, we will find them. The Jews are still here. They would not have had time to escape. More than likely, they are in Cairo. That's where I would be. They had help. We need to find out who it is."

"I am not sure what the situation is with the woman who worked for Hassan . . . Doria. Where is she? Is she dead? Is she one of them? I need to know what the hell is going on. How the hell did Hassan let this happen? I am embarrassed, actually humiliated, having the rockets and now they are dust! We must find them. How should we explain this to the world?"

CHAPTER TWENTY-SEVEN

HASSAN WAS LIKE A CAT WITH NINE LIVES. HE SENSED there was going to be retaliation by the Jews against his German facility. He felt there was little he could do to save it. The development of the research center and warehousing in Egypt made it easier for him to "write off" Germany. Now that he had the rockets and the technology to manufacture, his future was secure. The relationship and partnership with Nasser sealed a successful story.

Hassan did not hear firsthand of the disaster. He discovered it on German television while he was "avoiding" the boys from Tel Aviv. Needless to say, he was in a state of shock and his thoughts centered around the Jews. He, like Nasser, was feeling a sense of humiliation at being completely outsmarted by the Israelis. Naturally, his thoughts turned to Nasser. He had no defense. His security team was worthless and completely in shambles. Nasser would be out for blood, not only the Jews' but his. He had to tranquilize the situation. This could only be done in Egypt. Hassan picked up the phone and started to put a plan in motion.

Aron and Joshua had two major objectives. Number one, bring the threesome back to Israel alive; number two, get Hassan.

The safe house was located in downtown Cairo near the central plaza, Maydan Tahrir, close to everything including the commercial areas. It was exactly where everyone would not be searching. Nasr had used the apartment over the past two years for those who came over from the Company. It was on the top floor, and the apartment floor had heavy, padded carpeting. The windows had double blinds as well as shutters. The door was reinforced with steel bars. All the apartments in the building had bars on the windows, and the small terraces were encased with bars and mesh wire. Theft was a major factor, and the apartments were built like armored fortresses.

They chose it because it had access to the roof and could be used as an escape route if necessary. All the residences were connected so you were able to find a way to safety, building by building.

Nasr had a garage near the apartment, where he kept his own personal car. The stolen car had to be disposed of, but it would not be a problem, leaving it where it would be stolen again in hours. He wiped it clean for any prints and made sure nothing was left behind. Nasr had to get to his apartment and the office. He would be in touch.

The apartment had a phone, only to be used if there was an emergency. Nasr would ring three times, hang up, and then call again. They were exhausted as the adrenaline and the pressure just sapped their strength. All three just fell into bed, for the blinds were drawn and darkness prevailed.

Michael dreamed in color. The blasts came out of his subconscious with thundering noise that woke him from a deep sleep. He realized where he was and rolled over in an effort to find his dream, hoping the explosions had disappeared. Doria slept soundly. Her dreams were of Hassan and his fury. Bengy was just exhausted and dreamed of his native home in Haifa.

Nasser was organizing the most intense search in recent history. He wanted hourly reports and convened a meeting with his security organization and the directorate where Nasr worked. They divided the city into districts and planned to search the areas accordingly.

Aron and Joshua had returned to Israel and assembled "the brain trust" to come up with a plan to retrieve the threesome. It would not be easy given the amount of effort Nasser was putting into their capture.

They had penetrated Egypt with agents and paid informers. There was an Israeli network that was working. Because of the intense security effort by Nasser to find Michael and company, Aron and Joshua wanted to make sure their plans to retrieve them were well-thought-out. There were rewards for their capture, and they were dependent on Nasr to orchestrate any escape plan they put together.

Aron and Joshua were not forgetting Hassan. As far as they were concerned, he was living on borrowed time, but their focus was on Michael and company—bringing them back to Israel.

The loss of the two rockets was bad enough, but the whole research facility was gone. Dr. Deichman, the leading scientist, was a major casualty of the flood and explosions. He tried to escape the deluge and fell, hitting his head, and drowned. The entire program was set back years. Many of the German scientists that escaped the deluge had not the heart to continue. They opted to return to Argentina or Germany. The Egyptian experiment was over. Bengy's chess friends barely managed to stay alive and made plans to return to the fatherland.

Hassan had his connections and other identities that he used to find his way back to Cairo. He had to make peace with Nasser. They had a common goal and enemy. It was even more important now for both of them to recover and kill the Jews. Hassan was certain Michael was an Israeli spy along with the two technicians who had arrived later. He presumed Doria had fallen in love with Michael and went over to his side. He could not stand a traitor. He had given her everything, and this is how she repaid him.

He contacted a few of his security people and made plans to see what was left of his holdings. Hassan could not believe the devastation between the explosions, fire, and deluge. They had wiped out everything. His office had disappeared, as well as the warehouses, etc.

There were real problems. He owed large sums to his suppliers, and the inventory was gone, totally destroyed. Pressure for payment was not something to put aside. This world demanded payment on delivery or with a short credit window. He was in trouble, and it only made him more volatile, more determined to find them and administer pain.

He had lost almost everything in Germany and now here in Egypt. There were funds that he accumulated with the enormous profits made in the last year. Hassan was not about to lose this money. Negotiation would be needed to work out the outstanding invoices for the munitions. He believed it could be done.

There was still one substantial shipment in transit that he could turn into cash. That was not a "sure thing." Nasser was the recipient and would not pay because of the disaster. Things were not good. The shipment would have to be diverted to another client for cash payment.

Doria made coffee, and they sat at the kitchen table. They did not know what to say to each other. The room was dark, just slits of light sneaking through the cracks in the blinds. The plan for their escape had not been discussed before destroying the compound. All they knew was their escape would be in stages, and they were at stage one. The Company had to come up with stage two and beyond.

Michael assumed they would know a lot more when they saw Nasr in the evening. He would be privy to Nasser's plan to hunt them down. They were dependent on him to be the go-between with Tel Aviv. In the meantime, the day was upon them and there was little for them to do but worry.

Hassan finally made it to Nasser's office. There were harsh words between them, and the shouting could be heard down the halls. Then there were some fists slamming the desk, followed by a cold silence that settled over the office. They had come to a meeting of the minds. "Find them and kill them!"

Nasr was on his way after a long day putting his security force in place.

CHAPTER TWENTY-EIGHT

JOSHUA AND ARON HAD A DETAILED ESCAPE ROUTE
worked out for quite some time. They were not sure whether they
should put it into operation or consider another option. The threesome needed to be moved soon. Nasser and company had too much
manpower on the streets. They heard directly from Nasr the manhunt had more than one thousand agents scouring the city. He was
worried and pushed Tel Aviv to alter the plan. Eventually they would
find them. They felt they should move them as soon as possible. The
original plan was to use the Suez Canal as the escape route, getting
them to Ismailia, a city in northeastern Egypt with a population of
more than 750,000. It was situated on the West Bank of the Suez
Canal and the head office of the Suez Canal Authority was located
there. What Tel Aviv finally did not like about the scenario was
that it had a large contingent of the Muslim Brotherhood, allied
to Nasser. They were considering other courses of action. The lights
burned at the Company late into the night. There were a few dis-
agreements and some shouting, but they came to a unanimous decision. It was Alexandria.

They liked Alexandria because it was the second-largest city in
Egypt situated on the Mediterranean Sea and the largest seaport in
the country. They particularly liked that it was a significant tourist
destination with a sizable Coptic Christian population and many

churches. There would be more options open to them. What were the drawbacks? It was a logical place to try to leave the country and, therefore, drew added security.

The Company had a sophisticated network built in Alexandria. The sea offered numerous points for either leaving or entering the country. It was the perfect location to funnel their people into or out of Egypt. The network had two safe houses, one located in the city neighborhoods and one along the coast. Both were accessible to the sea. The most difficult problem facing Tel Aviv was how to move them from Cairo to Alexandria. It was only a two-hour drive at the most. More than likely, they would be brought to Israel by sea.

Nasser had shut down the airports and rail systems with his security details. The road was under heavy security but still seemed to be the best route. They devised a plan that would be difficult to uncover.

A truck would be sent from Alexandria to Cairo. It would have bills of lading for industrial chemicals being delivered to a Cairo factory. Tel Aviv also made out invoices for a return trip, transporting chemicals that were to go to the port of Alexandria for export. All the papers would be in order if it was stopped and searched, and likely that would occur.

The chemical drums were not the usual type for shipments. They had been designed with two sections. A top section would be utilized to store the supposed chemicals. The major section of the drum would be used to store a person. It would be cramped quarters. The trip, without issues, would take three hours. There would be twelve drums on the truck. Nine would be filled; the other three would hold the escapees. The truck driver would be one from the Company working in Egypt with proper papers. The stream of trucks carrying all types of materials to the port was commonplace from Cairo.

A lot of this had to be coordinated through Nasr. There was an established method of communication between Tel Aviv, Alexandria, and then to Cairo. The plan was put into effect.

Nasser's ring around Cairo tightened as they went from area to area searching entire neighborhoods. Hassan pressed Nasser for more personnel to search for the Jews. He felt the escape route went through Alexandria and personally used his own security organization to set up searches there. He had a command post in the center and laid out a strategy that could interact with Nasser's forces.

Nasr coordinated the move to Alexandria. The truck had no problem moving into the city. He moved his car out of the garage so they could make the switch in the darkness. All three entered the barrels and the top sections were filled with a mixture of water and a nontoxic chemical. The balance of the barrels were filled with regular chemicals that had been acquired and stored in the garage. It was a tight squeeze, but they were in and ready to go. They would have to endure the ride to their safe house, hopefully without incident.

The truck left around eight o'clock and headed for the highway. The traffic was crawling along. Up ahead, every vehicle, no matter what size or type, was being searched, as papers had to be verified.

The queue was endless, and the three-hour trip was becoming an ordeal for the three in the barrels. Finally, the truck came to the checkpoint and the police wanted to search the lorry. The driver presented his personal papers and the bills of lading and export licenses. They opened three barrels, none of which contained the escapees. Everything was working. The security force stamped the papers so they would not have a problem entering Alexandria. They would be stopped there, but the process would not include a major search since the papers were in order.

It was taking time, much longer than they anticipated. They were thankful for the ventilation. The truck made its way to Alexandria. As they expected, there was another checkpoint but not an outright search, as they had papers.

The barrels were becoming intolerable as the temperature approached 36° Celsius. They had taken precautions and brought water bottles, which literally saved them from dehydration. When they finally arrived, they could barely stand. Doria almost passed out and needed help getting out of the barrel. Michael and Bengy were completely wiped out. Everyone was pleased to have made it through the ordeal of escaping Cairo. They knew this was only a temporary reprieve, for what lay ahead would be the most difficult hurdle they would have to cross. The question in their minds was: "Can it be done?"

Alexandria had more than fifty very diverse neighborhoods with ethnic communities that had their own personalities, many with historical monuments, edifices, and public buildings. It had a population of more than three and a half million people. The consensus among the Company was to place the threesome in the Montaza section. It was located at the northeastern end of the city along the coast. There were 1.2 million people living in this district. The area included the neighborhood of Sidi Bishr, which was the summer resort site of the Egyptian middle class. It was summer, and the area was teeming with residents and day sunbathers wanting to be at the beach. The advantage was that both Michael and Doria both passed as Egyptians in every way. Bengy spoke Arabic, more as a Palestinian. They blended into any neighborhood. The safe house was fairly secluded and had a garage, as did Nasr's house.

They showered and found clothes left for them. Doria was in her hometown, where her mother lived. She had no idea what her mother knew about the situation. When she spoke with her about ten days before, Doria hinted that she might be taking a vacation. Doria was petrified that Hassan would take out his wrath on her, and he was very capable of doing so. It was impossible for her to even think of seeing her or calling.

The driver who brought them to Alexandria gave them a number to call if there was an emergency. He would reach them later in the day. As of the moment, there wasn't any definitive plan. That's all they were told.

They rested, Doria in Michael's arms. The events of the past seventy-two hours had taken their toll on them.

They lay in bed. "Michael, we haven't been this close in the past three weeks. What are you thinking?"

"I am just spent emotionally. We have been through the wringer together. We need to get out of this mess and get on with our lives. I am committed to our relationship more than ever. You are everything I desire and more. The question is: Do we have the strength to live through this assault on everything we strive to achieve in our lives? Will happiness, or should I say life itself, be part of our future? I would like it to happen. We certainly have earned the right to a life together. This test we are going through stands for everything we believe. You are about to leave your country, not knowing if you will ever be able to return. More so, maybe never seeing your mother again. You are giving up a life that two months ago only showed promise in every way. You will be going to a new country, culture, way of life because, as far as I can see, you have burned the bridge with Egypt. I have put you in such a difficult position, and I only hope that I am capable of delivering a life to you that will make this all worthwhile.

"We have caused pain, suffering, death, all in the name of right and freedom. We have to live with it and understand that what we have done must be a step forward for setting the record straight for keeping our corner of the world on the right path. We did what we did because we believed we were fighting evil in all its forms. History will bear that out, one way or another. There is nothing I would like to do more than thumb our noses at Hassan and Nasser." They laughed.

"You know, Michael Janssen, I love you and will follow you to the ends of the earth. I realize what I am doing. I felt your presence the first moment we met, and I knew we would find a life together. Sounds crazy . . . but it's true!

"It is hard to believe what has occurred. But through the course of all these events, I knew that we had to find a way to be together. I gave you all the reasons why I would consider leaving Egypt: ultra-nationalism, a dictatorship, anti-Semitism, and all the rest. They were important factors, but I am here because I feel I cannot live without you. Or should I say that life would not be what I wish without you. So, Michael, it all comes down to love, to live a life with you and our children. Nothing else really matters."

Michael smiled and hugged her. "My family will adore you!"

CHAPTER TWENTY-NINE

HASSAN WAS INCENSED WITH HATRED AND PUSHED HIS organization to search the city. He realized that Doria had been raised in Alexandria and knew her mother was alive. He made it his business to track her down and set up round-the-clock surveillance, hoping Doria would try to contact her. He tapped her phone, as he hoped they would make a mistake. Hassan had talked Nasser into allowing him to work with his security forces. The next step would be to hold Doria's mother hostage.

Nasser was not happy with Hassan. Allowing the destruction of his research facilities was an act that he could not forgive. When this was over, he would address it. His munitions, never mind the rockets, were gone. He had advanced him funds for shipments that were part of the explosion. The situation was not good, and his reputation in the Arab world was being questioned. He needed a victory and none was in sight, except finding the Jews.

The safe house had a view of the sea and the beach, which was filling up with vacationers and local residents. The area was in its season, for it was close to the height of the summer heat. The three-some did not move out of the house but were able to sit on a secluded veranda, sunshades half drawn. It would be difficult for anyone to actually see them. They presumed their rescue would come from the sea. It was the reason to be in Alexandria.

They had not heard a word and had seen very little of their contact. Before he left, he opened a locker and gave Michael and Bengy weapons. He hesitated with Doria, but Michael nodded and he gave her a weapon. They were Beretta model 70s, semiautomatic pistols that accommodated an eight-round magazine. Their weight was about seventeen ounces, and they had a three-and-a-half-inch barrel. It was a .22 caliber pistol, very compact, accurate, and a flawlessly reliable performer that could easily be used to quickly and accurately deliver multiple rounds to the body. It virtually had no recoil and could easily be controlled in rapid fire. It was the favorite of the Company because it was incredibly easy to operate, quickly allowing the slide to load the weapon. It was a fast way to empty the whole magazine. You could carry it with a fully loaded magazine and the chamber empty. They were fitted with silencers. Both Michael and Bengy were trained with the weapon. Michael showed Doria the basics. She had never held a gun, never mind fired one.

Aron and Joshua and their associates were finalizing the plans to bring them out.

The Egyptian Navy was on high alert. There were search parties patrolling the beach. Nasser had ordered twenty-four-hour surveillance along the coast. It was extensive coverage, never seen to this depth. Somehow, they had to find the time and place to snatch them from their pursuers. It seemed the search was centered in Alexandria. The amount of security agents and police had been doubled. Hassan was sold that they were here and had all his resources scouring the city and its outskirts.

Aron decided on a dramatic new plan. Surprise was everything! He believed they were asking too much to make an escape by sea. Israel did not have a submarine that could get close to the coast. A regular ship would be spotted from the air and destroyed. It was time to be creative.

They would leave by air. They would fly Cairo to Rome on a commercial flight. Michael would go as an Iraqi businessman in the textile business who traveled between Baghdad, Cairo, and Rome on a regular basis. His Iraqi dialect would lend credence to his identity. He would wear lightly tinted glasses and have a beard, hopefully his own. He was to fly first class while the others would be in economy. Doria's cover would be as a Catholic nun on assignment to the Vatican. This meant a new passport and papers for her reassignment. Bengy's new identity would be as a British Catholic priest. They would be traveling together. It would take days to put the plan into action, but the Tel Aviv group thought it was more than valid. They were betting that all the major searches were centered away from air travel. That would be assisted by Nasr, who would report that his information confirmed they were in Alexandria awaiting rescue by sea. The rumors and supposed sighting of the Jews heading to Alexandria reinforced the charade.

It meant going back to Cairo to Nasr rather than staying in Alexandria. The loop around the city was tightening as they left in the same truck and the same containers that had brought them. The truck was searched but not extensively. The lorry was opened just to see if the cargo looked legitimate. They would be at Nasr's almost four to five days in order to put the program together. They would need luggage with them. All of this had to be prepared. Alitalia would be the carrier. The flight was approximately three and a half hours to Fiumicino. They would be met in Rome by Aron and Joshua and brought to the Israeli embassy. Then plans would be made to bring them to Israel. There would be no other deviations from the plan. This was the final decision, and Rome was the destination. They thought of flying someone into Cairo and taking the flight with them back to Rome, but that didn't seem to be needed. The key factor was getting them through immigration and security. All their papers would be in order. There was added security everywhere. Michael would have business cards with an Iraqi address and phone number as well as the same information for his office in Italy. The Company set up a line so that if anyone called these numbers checking, they would be answered and handled in Tel Aviv. No stone was left unturned. They covered all the possibilities for failure. Even then they were uanable to guarantee success.The waiting was the killer, for it could not go by fast enough. All of these pieces would have to come together to find their way to Rome.

For all three, it was a time for taking inventory of themselves. They had managed to destroy the complex, defeat Hassan, and somehow stop Nasser for the time being. They now faced the problem of their own safety. Self-preservation was their goal. Could you blame them? The ordeal was much longer than they had dreamed, and sapped their inner strength.

Hassan was under immense pressure from all his resources and, naturally, from Nasser. His main thrust was to find the Jews, but he knew he had other pressing agendas in Germany and Switzerland that could not wait. He had to make plans to return to Europe even though he was obsessed with their capture. Nasser taunted him. He enjoyed seeing this German, for he was really a German not one of them, be on the brink of a breakdown and financial ruin. He would recover and find another way, but Hassan was a necessary casualty in his estimation. He would lick his wounds and live to fight another day. Nasser had other plans that did not include

Hassan. They centered around the Russians. They were his way out of this dilemma.

Tel Aviv knew this win was only temporary. It was a major delaying action. The drums of war were still beating, and it was still necessary to keep the swords sharpened for another day. The defeats only heightened the possibility of future conflicts. The concensus was that it was only a temporary reprieve. The Company was worrying about a wounded adversary still able to fight. They were the worst kind.

Tel Aviv was proud and surprised that Michael and crew had pulled it off. They were relieved they didn't have to bomb and create an international incident. Nasser was embarrassed, telling the press that it was an accident that caused the explosion.

Hassan was on their most-wanted list. He had caused them great pain and losses with his sale of weaponry to Israel's enemies. They had destroyed his factories, but that was not enough. They didn't want him to be able to fight another day.

He had gone back to Egypt, at least for the time being. They preferred not to assassinate him in Europe because of all the adverse publicity. But that was not a deterrent. If Europe was the only place he could be eliminated, so be it. His weaponry had blown up busses in Jerusalem, produced explosions in the streets of Europe, and killed many innocent people throughout the Middle East and Africa. He was a marked man for extinction, and Aron and Joshua were his trackers.

Hassan knew he had to disappear as soon as he could put all his finances in order. It would be off to Germany first and then to Switzerland as soon as he had a chance to kill these Jews. His German superior attitude was waning. He was still in shock over the events and how to deal with them, for Europe beckoned as quickly as possible.

The preparations for their exodus from Egypt were taking longer than expected. In a way, they were asking the Red Sea to part. Getting everything right, absolutely right, was complicated! Michael paced the apartment waiting for the go-ahead. Doria was tearful, thinking of her mother and family and knowing she may never see Egypt again. Nasr had to go to work every day. He would return on some evenings when it was early enough for them to talk at length. He was pretty certain he was above suspicion. No one linked him to the Jews, the explosions, or his spying for Israel.

Finally, they were ready. The flight had been booked and the disguises, luggage, and clothing were in place. They were set to go! It was an early morning flight, leaving Cairo at 8:30 in the morning. It meant an early arrival and check-in at the airport. Nasr arranged for two cars to take the passengers. The cars and drivers came from Alexandria, for no one else could be trusted. Even this early in the morning, three hours before flight time, the airport was alive with people. The activity was close to capacity. The flight was selected exactly for this reason. Michael went alone, ten minutes after Bengy and Doria. Nasr hugged each of them. There was not much to say, for they were brothers in arms. There was now a bond between them forever. They had faced the enemy and prevailed.

It was somewhat ironic. The Prime Minister of Italy, Amintore Fanfani, was arriving later in the day for a state visit with Nasser. He was coming primarily for a trade mission. Added security was already set up at the arrivals area and that section of the airport. Security would be focused on the arriving dignitary. Nasser would be there to meet him.

The airport was located in Heliopolis, about seventeen miles from the center where Nasr lived. Even at that wee hour of the morning, traffic was heavy. Doria and Bengy arrived first and were assaulted by boys wanting to carry their suitcases. Bengy was there shooing them away and took both cases and entered the terminal. There was already a significant line of passengers in the queue, just to get into the correct line for flights. There appeared to be a queue to verify that everyone had a ticket, apparently some sort of security check on anyone entering. Bengy and Doria were shown some courtesy and were directed to the correct check-in station. They stood in line for quite some time until they got to the Alitalia ticket agent. Seats were assigned, passports were checked, and they were given boarding passes. They were then directed to the immigration lines, where the real test would take place. They could see up ahead that each passenger was being grilled by a team of security people. Bengy, as the monsignor, and Doria, as Sister Maria, performed well. They each gave a credible story of their mission to Rome, showing their papers and documentation from the Church. They were searched. Their luggage was completely opened and every item was examined.

Michael went through the same process, but as a first-class passenger, there was much less of a queue and commotion. The amenities of first class started there. As he had requested, he was assigned a seat at the rear of the first-class cabin. A quick check of his passport, and he was given clearance to the security and immigration area.

In his Iraqi dialect, he explained his presence in Cairo, showed his hotel bill and business cards that he acquired during his trip. As he had anticipated, they asked him several questions about Iraq. They questioned him about why he was going to Rome. He told them of his office and visiting resources. One of his interrogators asked if they could call his office for verification. He replied they could do so but the office did not open until ten in the morning. It was written on the card. "Well, it is later in the morning in Baghdad. Can we call there? Are they open?"

"Yes, of course. We open much earlier there. The number is on my card. I am not sure who is in this early, but someone should answer."

The agent reached for the phone looking for a reaction from Michael. "I don't think that will be necessary. You are cleared."

It took time to replace everything in his suitcase. They had inspected every article. He was like a spring stretched to its limit, ready to snap. Slowly he started to realize that he could now let up.

Michael decided not to go into the first-class lounge but sat in the waiting area with the rest of the economy-class passengers. It was a full flight in economy. It seemed everyone wanted to go to Rome.

He could see Doria and Bengy sitting five or six rows to his right in the lounge. He did not acknowledge them in any way. As far as he was concerned, the ordeal was not over until the plane was out of Egyptian airspace. The pressure was excruciating.

He picked up his paperback novel in Arabic and pretended to be deeply absorbed. He thought of getting a newspaper but did not want to walk around and possibly be recognized by any of the security forces.

Boarding would not take place for at least thirty-five minutes. First class would board first, which would ease some of his tension. Anything could happen until that plane got off the ground. His thoughts went to Hannah, Rachel, and Abe and Sarah, whom he considered family. He knew they were worried, as they had not heard from him in some time. He could not concentrate. There was a slight delay in boarding, and it seemed like an eternity. They finally announced it, and he lost track of the other two as he entered the jetway to the first-class cabin. He was somewhat at ease knowing that Doria and Bengy were cleared to board.

"Buongiorno, Senor Habib, welcome to Alitalia. Here is your seat. Enjoy the flight." It was the last row in the first-class cabin on the right-hand side as he entered. Michael sat next to the window. He did not know if the aisle seat would be occupied. He hoped it would be empty. The Company had also bought it.

Doria and Bengy joined the throngs in the queue to board. They were sitting in the same seats one row ahead of each other. With Bengy's help, Doria's small flight bag as well as his went in the overhead.

They were seated in the Italian section, and all they heard was Neapolitan dialect. A large group of Italian tourists was returning and wanted to change seats to sit with family and friends. This happened on a regular basis, so the flight attendant just threw up her hands. Organization was not a strength of Italians. It was not normal unless there were hostile and heated discussions over the seating. Doria was asked to move one seat over, and that completed a complicated exchange.

The air-conditioning was not working full force, and Doria's habit and Bengy's collar were not helping the situation. Michael, at the same time, told the stewardess he wanted to rest, refused the welcome drink and breakfast, and turned to the window and feigned sleep while waiting for takeoff.

CHAPTER THIRTY

HASSAN HAD MADE THE DECISION THE NIGHT BEFORE TO leave Egypt. He made last-minute reservations to fly to Rome and then on to Munich, as he could not get a nonstop to Germany. The traffic through Alexandria to the Cairo airport was impossible, and he made the flight as the doors on the aircraft were closing. He was seated in the first-class section about nine rows from Michael on the opposite aisle. When he boarded, he was exhausted from running for the flight. If he did not have VIP status with the Egyptian security, he wouldn't have made the flight. He slumped into his seat and started to collect himself.

The aircraft lifted off and within minutes was over the sea. All three felt the weight of the world was off their shoulders. Michael surprisingly fell asleep. Hassan and Michael were no more than thirty feet from one another. It was only a three-and-a-half-hour flight. What were the chances of them meeting in the aisle or restroom? If you thought about it, the scene was from a Marx Brothers movie, two adversaries back-to-back stalking around in circles or something like that, not knowing where the other one was. What could or would they do if they met?

Michael and Hassan had empty seats next to them, for the cabin was about three-quarters full. Breakfast was served, but they both declined and slept. The flight was fairly smooth and uneventful, keeping both parties sleeping. The Alitalia staff went about their business serving the passengers. Michael got up and used the restroom directly behind him and returned to his seat, totally unaware of who was sitting thirty feet away.

Hassan had not slept the night before and did not stir during the entire flight. He had nightmares, dreaming of being chased by the Jews around the Great Sphinx. Doria and Bengy closed their eyes, but the endless chatter of the Neapolitans made sleep impossible.

The announcement blared from the loudspeaker. "Fasten your seat belts and prepare for landing." They were twenty minutes from Fiumicino, and there was some turbulence going through the low-lying clouds. The plane began its approach. The wheels descended with a shriek and they were minutes from touching down.

Michael was up and awake. A calm had settled over him as he saw the ground rushing up toward him. They felt the usual jolt as they touched down amidst the clapping and chants of "Bravo" by the contingent from Naples. The glide to the gate took about six to eight minutes, and everyone stayed in their seats while they prepared to embark. Soon they were at the gate and the seat belt light went off. There was the usual ping signaling it was all right to get out of your seat and head to the exit. First class always embarked first. The stewardesses held back economy class until everyone in the up-front cabin had left. Michael got up and opened the overhead bin and took out his briefcase with his back to the cabin. He turned around to head out, as he was very close to the exit.

Looking across the aisle, he could not believe who he was seeing. Hassan stood and started up the opposite aisle. There were passengers ahead of him, so he was waiting for them to head for the exit.

Either he didn't see Michael or didn't recognize him because of his disguise with glasses and a beard.

Michael was stunned, totally in shock. Should he attack him, confront him, or do nothing? This was Italy, not Egypt. He felt frozen but had to move, for there were passengers in the aisle that wanted to leave the aircraft. He turned the corner toward the exit and made eye contact with Hassan. The look on Hassan's face was that of horror, fear, and, most of all, madness all at the same time. He, as it was with Michael, did not know what to do. This was not Egypt, nor was he in an advantageous position. There had to be Israelis waiting for him. Were they here where they exit or at customs? His instincts were to escape and not get into a confrontation at this time. They were headed toward the passport-control booths, each watching each other's every move.

Michael was at full speed. "Where is he going? Why is he here?"

Hassan was thinking, "Can I make the flight to Munich? Will I be able to avoid these Jews until I get on the plane?"

Michael was trying to think ahead. "Aron and Joshua will meet us when we exit customs. How can I reach them before that?" Finally, he saw Doria and Bengy in the passport-control line. He motioned to them to look to their right. They could see Hassan in the line. Doria spotted him first and almost cried out "Oh, my God!" Bengy caught her and kept her upright. Hassan went through passport control much faster than the threesome. He had a German passport, which allowed him to move through controls more quickly. Michael saw him turn toward the area marked "connecting flights."

Hassan looked at the board to see where and when his flight would be available. It was late, almost two hours. He had to make a decision. Should he wait or change plans and stay in Rome?

He found a phone booth and called the German embassy. "Is Heinrich Mueller in? Please connect me. It is Hassan. It is urgent."

"Heinrich, I am here in Rome and I need your help. It is imperative. I am calling in a favor. We have helped each other in the past. I need your official car to pick me up at Fiumicino and a room in the embassy for a night or two." They decided on a time and place.

Michael's luggage arrived quickly because it was marked "priority." He told Doria and Bengy he was heading out of the customs area to find Aron and Joshua. The boys were there when Michael came out through the swinging doors. They could not believe it when Michael blurted it out. They rushed to the phones, checking the flights to Germany and calling Tel Aviv to see if they could get specific information on Hassan's flight plans. In the meantime, Doria fell into the arms of Michael, crying uncontrollably. They were tears of joy and finality.

The German embassy was located on the Via San Martino della Battaglia. It had eleven other consulates throughout Italy. Rome was staffed with more than five hundred diplomatic representatives. Mueller was s senior member of the embassy and had extreme right-leaning views and a connection with the Third Reich at one time. Hassan was picked up and taken there. His new itinerary and situation were the topics of discussion.

Michael had other business. He called Hannah and told her he was in Rome. His schedule was still up in the air, but he was safe and would give her his itinerary over the next week. She was relieved, and although she wanted to know more, she did not ask. He then placed a call to Abe and Sarah. It was still the middle of the night in Boston, but he wanted them to know he was alive and well. They wanted to know everything, especially when he would return.

"I will call you this coming week with more information."

Doria did not let go of him. She hung on to him for dear life. The whole situation had drained her. Bengy called Haifa and spoke with his parents. With Hassan on the loose, the boys wanted the threesome to stay at the Israeli embassy located on Via M. Mersati.

It took a while to figure out that Hassan did not make a connecting flight. He did not board the flight to Munich or any other flight. He was somewhere in Rome or Italy. Hassan was headed eventually for his money, more than likely to Switzerland, but somehow or another, he had to get to his safe deposit boxes.

Everyone was at the Israeli embassy with a joyous feeling in the air, for they had prevailed over Nasser. The objective was attained. They managed to escape injury and certain death.

Hassan could not believe the course of events, but he was a realist. He wanted his money, a new identity, and more than likely a new country. He needed to get to Munich first to retrieve certain documents and then on to Zurich. Most of all, he wanted revenge. Sneaking away was not in his plans; not now, especially the way things happened.

Heinrich told him the Jews were at the Israeli embassy. His people watched who came and went.

"Heinrich, I know you have always been a believer in the Third Reich and have worked to defeat the Jews. I want to put a plan together that will revenge all our work in Egypt. I will pledge all my resources to see that it will happen. Money is not an issue. My priority at first was setting up a new identity. Now that has changed. I want their heads!"

CHAPTER THIRTY-ONE

ARON AND JOSHUA DID NOT WANT TO PRESS ALL THREE for their story. Too much had gone on today. They would pick it up in the morning. The conversation among them was about Hassan, who more than likely was in Rome formulating his movements. They were not without information. Their informant told them a new person was being "entertained" at the German embassy.

Over his cappuccino, Heinrich laid out some ideas that involved retaining additional personnel for their plan.

Hassan spoke up. "They are destined for Israel. If we want them, now will be our best opportunity when they depart for their flight. Do we kill them or do we want them alive? That's the major question. Either one can be accomplished. We will need to plan quickly. I believe they will be here at least two days or more. I will know more by noon time today."

"There will be a fee either way you decide."

Michael was adamant. "I am not going to Israel until we find this bastard. This business is not finished until I see this guy dead or captured. It has now become personal."

It was a unanimous decision among all of them. Tel Aviv had already given their blessing to Aron and Joshua.

228

Aron spoke first. "We now know that he is in the German embassy. We thought that was the case, but we have now confirmed it. Hassan eventually has to leave, and we will find him."

Michael broke in. "We want a great Italian meal. I suggest the five of us go out to dinner. I haven't had a decent meal in five weeks!"

Both sides were preparing for war on Roman soil, not knowing what the other was planning and unaware they knew the whereabouts of each other.

Michael always liked Tuscan food, especially since he hadn't enjoyed a good meal for quite a while. They went to a Florentine restaurant on the top of the Via Veneto called Toscana. Between the antipasto, pasta, and Bistecca Fiorentina, the meal more than made up for the weeks in Egypt.

Tel Aviv had given them the go-ahead. Hassan was in their sights, and two of their best agents were there to get the job done. While the five of them devoured their meals at the dinner table, men from the embassy stood guard.

Michael was persistent.

"Aron, we want our Berettas back if we are going to be part of this manhunt. Besides, he is after us also. I can feel it. This is not a negotiable point. How do we get to him?"

Joshua chimed in. "He wants to get to Germany and Switzerland. We do not know which one first. Hassan needs his hands on his money, and I believe other passports exist in his safety deposit box that will allow him to travel with a new identity.

We cannot let him out of Europe or assume a new identity. He has friends and allies here in the German embassy who are more than willing to help him. Many of them are from the Fascist movement.

He is desperate, and no one is more dangerous than when he knows his life is on the line.

"We need to smoke him out of the embassy so we can capture or kill him. He wants to kill all three of you, and we have to give him the opportunity, but on our terms. Let's put our heads together and see what are our options. Until now, our constant study of the situation caused us to change plans for the better. Let's keep that ability to turn over every stone and come up with the answers."

They all started to speak at the same time, which resulted in laughter.

They wanted to create a story that Michael and company were now not affiliated with Tel Aviv and wanted no part of any further issues involving Israel and Egypt. This was possible by letting information leak to some of the administrators at the German embassy. They were planning a trip to Florence, where Michael's mother would meet them, as she was on a tour of Europe.

They chose Firenze, as they could control the physical aspects of the city much better. The story sounded plausible. Any calls to check on Hannah would be transmitted to their people to cover the story. It was a good plan, but it had its drawbacks. They did not want to risk a major confrontation in Rome. Being the capital and the home of all the embassies and the Vatican, it would make the news coverage, good or bad, much greater than it was. One way or another, Hassan was not going to elude them.

The threesome would be the bait. The question was: would Hassan go fishing? They believed he couldn't resist!

Florence was a three-and-a-half-hour drive on the Autostrada. They could take the train, but it would give Hassan more of an advantage. Michael knew the city. It was part of his education with

Abe and Sarah, going to the Italian fashion shows and working with their resources close to Florence for footwear and accessories. The idea of showing Doria the city excited him.

Aron and Joshua, in order to trap Hassan, realized they needed additional personnel from Tel Aviv. He had outfoxed them on two earlier occasions. Five agents and Avrom arrived, flying into Rome. Joshua wanted them in place in Florence so there would be zero chance of Hassan's escape. The threesome was booked into the Park Palace Hotel. It was a small hotel, set back from the street away from the traffic. It was situated in a secluded spot just off the Viale Michelangelo, with aged stone walls in a country setting. The hotel was run by a Swiss family and considered an out-of-the-way hideaway for clandestine lovers. The hotel was perfect for their purposes. It was away from other neighborhoods and the city in general.

Next to the main building was a separate two-story villa annex. Michael and Doria would stay on the second floor and Bengy and the new agents would be on the ground floor.

Aron and Joshua had made a number of reservations, hoping to stay in the same hotel as Hassan, but if that couldn't be achieved, they would stay up the road at the Villa Cora, which was less than a mile away. They decided it was the best location. Hannah was not coming, for in her place was a female agent impersonating her. She was booked into the main building.

Hassan received the information from Heinrich, and they were more than suspicious. The Jews were not on a pleasure trip but on a hunting expedition, and the prey was Hassan. Even though it could be a trap, he could not resist the chance to kill them. He would find a way, enlisting certain help that was essential.

Heinrich made a call to Munich and five associates arrived the next day. In Hassan's mind, it came down to a question of wills. "I will prevail!"

Michael felt this would bring about closure one way or another. He couldn't wait to get his hands on Hassan. However, spending his life with Doria chasing him around Europe was not in his plans. It would end here in Florence or he would let Tel Aviv find him.

Michael had fond memories of Florence. His first trip was with Abe and Sarah to the fashion shows on a buying/product-development trip. He had walked almost every inch of the city during his four-day stay. Everything was so new, so interesting, so exciting. He was captured by his Florentine experience. "Someday, I will be back with the love of my life."

Now, here he was again! The circumstances were not what he had bargained for, but he was here with Doria, trying to find some enjoyment together. Michael wanted to show her the *David*, the Ponte Vecchio, the Pitti Palace, and to be the tour guide.

Hassan stayed in the city at the Berchielli. He chose the hotel because it had two entrances, one on the Lungano, the other on a winding back-alley street. It had what you would call a piazzetta. He paid the hotel to have his car there with a guard. Sitting on the seat was an automatic weapon.

In a sense, it was like Wyatt Earp against the Clampetts in a fight at the OK Corral. The tension and the drama were building as both sides put plans into action.

It was not easy, but Aron and Joshua tracked down Hassan and his hotel. They had to admit he had made the perfect choice, especially with the ability to have a car at his beck and call. It would be a game of chess played out in the heart of the Renaissance, the home of the Medicis and Machiavellis. The chess pieces were dangerous, for they brought revenge and death. Someone in this fabled city would die.

Doria had never been to Italy, never mind Florence, and she was mesmerized by its beauty and history. They were here to kill Hassan, but in the process of bringing him out in the open, they had an opportunity to see the city.

Michael wanted to walk the city. Aron and Joshua had a program for him. As he and Doria were the bait, they had to orchestrate the right itinerary for him, for along the route would be the men from Tel Aviv. "Hannah" had arrived, and they wanted the three of them to stroll toward the Duomo along a specific path, Via Maggio.

Bengy and Avrom were now part of the reconnaissance team. They were the only ones, besides Michael and Doria, who were able to recognize Hassan. They drove down to Porta Romana and started to walk into the city on Via Maggio, reaching the Ponte S. Travita Bridge over the Arno. They were entering the more fashionable part of the city, crossing in front of Ferragamo. Their walk was in the direction of the Ponte Vecchio. They were covered every step of the way, walking right past the Berchielli's Lungano entrance.

Michael stopped and entered a shop he had known from his other two trips. Alessi was owned by a wonderful couple, Roberto and Anna. They greeted him like their long-lost son and welcomed Doria and Hannah's undercover as well. Michael bought some shirts and trousers and Doria ended up with four to five outfits. They did not have much to wear since Egypt. Everything was, in a sense, almost normal, but the idea that Hassan and associates could be firing at them any moment hung over their thoughts. Everyone was on guard.

Doria was enchanted with the Ponte Vecchio and captivated by the magnificent jewelry. Their tour moved on to Piazza Signoria, Palazzo Vecchio, and the *David* and ended at the Duomo. It was enough for today.

They took taxis back to the Park Palace while the Company people picked up the car at Porta Romana. They had tested the waters and shown they were in Florence. Hassan's people reported back to him with all the details.

They made plans for dinner at Omero's, which was further in the hills of Tuscany, across the street from the House of Gallileo. It was famous for what they called "flattened chicken" on the grill with vegetables and roasted potatoes.

They drank wine and even laughed. Michael looked at Doria and visualized a new life with this woman. "She loves me, God knows why! She has given up a life in Egypt for me. How can I ever make her happy? She has made her lot with our people. This woman is the essence of my life."

Hassan now had Michael's location and thought it would be best to bring the war to him. He sent two of his people to scout out the grounds of their hotel. They had the layout and knew exactly where the Jews were staying in the attached villa. The hotel was out of the way and the surroundings were wooded. It was next to Forte Belvedere where the fantastic oversized sculptures of Henry Moore were on display. It was a fort that was built to protect the center of government in Florence, the Pitti Palace, and the south end of the city. The Medicis built the fort to show their power and status.

Hassan felt he had several options for an attack and clean getaway. The more he went over the plan, the more he liked it. He thought the advantage would be his, for they would not expect an attack at the hotel. The plan was daring but sound.

Aron and Joshua were very concerned, for they now knew Hassan was staffed up, which meant only one thing: he would go on the offensive. They gathered those from Tel Aviv and put together a plan of action.

Hassan and company in the dead of the night. They were professionals, most likely alumni of the Waffen SS. The telephone lines were their first objective. They were all in black, armed to the teeth with Russian weapons. In their belts they carried Stechkin machine pistols with silencers, and over their shoulders, they had AK-74s with night scopes and many clips. They wanted to use German guns, but they were not available.

The Park Palace had iron gates that were closed after midnight. If you wanted to enter, you would use the intercom and the night attendant would buzz you in. There was a stone circular drive leading to the main building with a fountain in the center. The villa where Michael and company were staying was off to the left. It was a rather large residence done in Tuscan stucco with louvered wooden shutters that were closed for the night.

The edges of the property were drawn by the growth of bushes and trees that formed a natural barrier. There was a road leading to a pathway for Forte Belvedere.

It was not the perfect night for a raid. The moon was at its brightest and the temperature did not drop off significantly to cool one down. Dressed in black with grease paint on their faces was not an asset, for they were sweating profusely. They wanted to eliminate the Israeli guard who patrolled the hotel grounds.

Aron and Joshua had constant communication from their hotel to the Park Palace. They did not want to stay at the Park Palace. They wanted to have the flexibility if there was an attempt on the three-some. Two agents were always on duty when the gates were closed. Every night they set up trip wires to give them those extra seconds. They were located in key positions around the grounds. The area around the main building was well lit. The strategy was to position the Mercedes near the villa for quick access if necessary.

There were now five additional well-armed Israeli agents, not including Bengy and Avrom, and the woman agent rounded out the defenders. This did not include Michael and Doria, who were armed with Berettas and Uzi submachine guns.

On the right side of the grounds, next to the hotel, was a small structure with large windows. It was used as a small office. One agent was always there and had an unobstructed view of the gates.

CHAPTER THIRTY-TWO

HASSAN'S PLAN WAS STRAIGHTFORWARD, WITH AN option. Number one, they wanted to create a blitzkrieg. The plan was to procure a truck and ram through the gates. It would carry his team into action and create an advantage. Number two, they could infiltrate the hotel grounds and attack the guard house and the main target, the villa.

They stole the biggest truck they could find. It was more than capable of breaking through the hotel gates. Hassan liked the idea, and if it did not work, they had brought industrial clippers to cut the chains.

Aron and Joshua took turns on duty. One was always up to communicate or go into action. The Villa Cora was one of the most beautiful, elegant hotels in Florence, just minutes from the Park Palace.

Hassan and friends boarded the truck on the other side of the Arno. One of his confederates had "borrowed" it the day before near the Stazione Centrale. They wound their way to Porta Rome and stopped to go over the last details before ascending Viale Michelangelo.

It was a hot, humid night, and both Michael and Doria were not sleeping well. They were in each other's arms, just lying there cherishing the moment. Michael got up to get some San Pellegrino from the small refrigerator that decorated every hotel room in Italy.

They were wide-awake and sat on the edge of the bed, drinking from the same glass.

Hassan stopped the truck again about a hundred meters from the hotel entrance to double check their weapons. At this time of the morning, there was almost no traffic; just an occasional motorcycle could be heard. Everyone was sweating.

They revved up the engine and pushed for maximum speed to break through the gates. The force of the truck broke the chains and threw down two-thirds of the cast-iron fence. It sounded like a sonic boom as the fence and a portion dragged under the chassis. Hassan's men jumped into action as soon as they were through the gates. There were bullets flying, aimed at cutting down two guards on duty.

Michael jumped off the bed, threw his pants and shoes on, and grabbed his weapons. Doria dressed quickly and took out her Beretta. They were upstairs in the villa and knew they were the reason for all this firing. Michael was unsure what to do. Should he try to get out of the villa and find a way into the wooded area with Doria? He hesitated to do this as he opened the shutters and prepared to fire.

Hassan wanted them dead, and he was about to move heaven and earth to make it happen. All the agents on the first floor were already in action.

All the lights went on everywhere in the hotel and then went off. Most guests were looking for hiding places. The two Israeli guards were returning fire, but one was wounded. The balance of the contingent had the shutters open, firing away.

Hassan was directing the group with a walkie-talkie from behind the truck. The Germans did not expect to run into such heavy resistance. One of them had set off a trip wire and was blown up by the charge that was live.

Aron and Joshua were already in the car only three minutes away from the entrance.

The Hassan forces were well prepared. They threw smoke grenades into the villa and caused havoc with the Israelis. A ladder appeared, and they were able to scale the roof and shoot their AKs through the roof, which sent the bullets into the living quarters.

Michael emptied a clip into the roof, hoping to hit the assailants. He didn't know if he was successful, as he couldn't see very well through the smoke. It was becoming almost impossible to stay there between the smoke and the flying projectiles.

He took Doria by the arm. "I am behind you and will tug your shirt, so please realize I am there. Do not leave me!"

They worked their way down the stairway and stayed in the small hall, deciding whether to make a run for the main house, the car, or the shrubbery. It was probably one of the most important decisions of his life.

Aron and Joshua had arrived. They left the car at the entrance and had their Uzis ready. Joshua started shooting at some of the Germans who were using the stone wall and sitting area for cover. They did not know if any were killed but thought some of the assailants were wounded.

The intense fire into the first floor of the villa was doing its job. There were casualties, and the return fire had lessened. It didn't seem intense, in a sense, as most of the weapons being fired had silencers.

Michael felt his best option was to make it through the shrubbery down a road into Forte Belvedere. There were numerous hiding places that came to mind. The oversized sculptures would serve their purpose. There was a bit of a no-man's-land they had to cross, but it seemed to be the best course of action. Michael realized he had to move now or they would be in harm's way. He explained the plan to Doria and they were both ready to move.

Hassan was only interested in finding Michael. As far as he was concerned, the casualties did not matter. He wanted Michael's life and his Egyptian whore.

"OK, on a count of three, we will run into the shrubbery about twenty meters away. Don't look back, just run as fast as you can. I will be behind you firing."

Aron and Joshua were trying to eliminate the opposition. They had outflanked them, and the Germans were now caught in crossfire. It was taking its toll.

Hassan spotted them running and motioned to one of his cohorts to follow. It was time to kill them.

Michael and Doria ran into the bushes and made it to the access road to Forte Belvedere. He felt they had a good chance to evade Hassan's crew in the park, using the sculptures to their advantage. The sculptures were magnificent and seemed to come to life in the moonlight. Michael and Doria were exhausted from the run and stopped to catch their breath, sitting on a small sculpture that had flat surfaces. There wasn't a sound until they heard pings causing some stone chips to fly.

The fort served Michael and Doria's purpose. However, dawn would soon be upon them, eliminating some of their cover. Michael had his Beretta and still had his Uzi but was on his last clip. They wove in and out of the massive pieces of stone, hoping they could hide from their pursuers.

Hassan and his associate were following, sending volleys of bullets wherever they thought they were hiding.

The light would be coming soon, and that would be to Michael and Doria's disadvantage. They were stalked by Hassan and a attacker., Michael knew they were better shots than he and Doria. He could take the path that went down almost to the Ponte Vecchio, but he would be giving them a clearer shot. Doria was tiring, and Michael had to put them on the defensive, at least make them less aggressive until help came.

"I am going to try to outflank them. I want you to move back and forth between these two sculptures, only stay in this area. I will try to circle behind them." Doria did not want to leave Michael's side but agreed.

Michael was on target and got off two shots with the Beretta that hit the associate. It did not kill him, but he was out of action. Hassan picked up his AK and started spraying bullets everywhere. He was furious.

Michael doubled back to make sure Doria was not hit and was functioning. She was more than shaken; she was falling apart. He hugged her. "It's OK. We are in decent shape. Hassan has lost his man. Let's keep doing what we are doing."

CHAPTER THIRTY-THREE

ARON, JOSHUA, AND THEIR AGENTS HAD CHOSEN THE right strategy. They had circled Hassan's "army" and were slowly destroying them. Out of the six men, two were dead, two were slightly wounded, and two were still firing but ready to bail out. They weren't ready to die for Hassan. It was not the Third Reich they were fighting for.

Hassan was not interested in helping his wounded comrade. He was going to kill the Jew any way he could. He was about to throw caution to the wind just as the Western bad man comes out blazing with both barrels. His strategy was actually working.

Michael's Uzi jammed and his eyes were on Doria as well. He literally picked her up and put her under his arm, maneuvering around another statue.

Hassan was finding the range, and bullets were coming very close to both Michael and Doria. He had thrown away the AK and was firing with the pistol. The whole situation seemed surreal. Bullets were flying, but there was hardly a noise coming from the silencers on the weapons. Hassan rushed while changing the clip and the Russian machine pistol jammed. The weapon had that reputation.

Michael saw what was happening and realized he was only fifteen to twenty meters from Hassan. He didn't have to think. Without hesitating, he sprinted to him in record time. He tackled him right in the midsection as Hassan still held his weapon. Michael reached out and knocked the pistol from his grasp. They rolled around, each trying to gain the necessary leverage to get an advantage.

Doria was horrified and for a moment frozen with fear. She desperately wanted to help and searched for her weapon she had dropped somewhere near the sculptures. Her only option was to try to beat Hassan with her fists as they wrestled on the ground. She was swatted away with a tremendous blow to the body that sent her tumbling.

They fought for what seemed like hours, and both were exhausted. Hassan reached out and found the used AK he had discarded, using it as a club. Michael had to let go of him, for the blows were taking their toll. He backed off and tried to find a weakness in Hassan's attack. He was bloodied and losing his strength.

Hassan saw he had the opportunity to send out a death blow. As he raised the weapon, a shot rang out that hit him directly in the head. He was dead before he hit the ground.

Out of the shadows Bengy walked over to Michael, his Beretta in hand. The threesome embraced! There were tears of joy, exhaustion, and definitely closure.

Aron and Joshua arrived about the same time. They wanted to get all concerned out of the fort and out of Italy.

They now had to win the last battle and not get caught! The key was to get things cleaned up. There were people from the embassy in Rome who had arrived to help. Within twenty minutes of the battle, nothing was left on the ground. They were fortunate the telephone lines had been cut so that the hotel was isolated. All the weapons fired had silencers, which had created a noise level that could only be heard in the complex. The grounds were many meters from the street in an area not inhabited. Forte Belvedere was secluded. It was the main reason they chose the Park Palace.

Everyone was in sedans on the Autostrada heading to Pisa to catch the flight to London. There was a private aircraft waiting, already cleared with a flight plan to the UK. The embassy people were on their way to Rome with the bodies for disposal. The Germans who surrendered were driven to Verona and then up the Autostrada to the Brenner Pass and left there for their "cousins" to pick them up.

Naturally, there was an investigation, but with no physical evidence except bullet holes in the concrete, it was only a presumption of what had occurred.

There was the question of how to handle Hassan's departure. The German government wanted to know what happened to him. They pressed Tel Aviv, who gave them the story that Hassan more than likely was killed in the explosion of the underground illegal facility. It would be impossible to identify his body. He had used a false identity on the trip from Cairo to Rome so there wasn't any record of his entering Europe.

Nasser was more concerned with the loss of the rockets and the German scientists. This was an embarrassment that was difficult to cover up. Nasser pinned the blame on Hassan's operations, which caused him to perish in the explosions. Tel Aviv could not have planned it better.

CHAPTER THIRTY-FOUR

IT WAS LONDON TO TEL AVIV AFTER FIVE DAYS AT THE
London embassy. They owed the British and Americans for their
support and giving the operation credibility. Behind the scenes help
from M15 and the CIA was critical to the success of the mission.

Michael and Doria were both debriefed. It covered every part of
the operation. There were some interesting points that resulted from
the operation, besides the destruction of the rockets and research
facility.

#1 Israel still had to face a possible Pan-Arab alliance.
#2 Nasser, although wounded, was still dangerous, pos-
sibly more so.
#3 Israel had escaped a nightmare. Would it possibly reoccur?

Doria gave them a different perspective on Hassan's operations.
All in all, the amount of information that came forth made a dramatic difference to the three security groups.

When they finally arrived in Israel, they were surprised to find
Hannah, Rachel, Abe, and Sarah! Abe had called the prime minister
and, in his words, asked "What the hell is going on with Michael?"
The prime minister told him he was safe in London and on his way

to Israel. Abe flew the entire family there so they could greet him and thank everyone for his safe return.

Hannah and Rachel had never been to Israel and, naturally, were there primarily to see Michael. Hannah had another agenda, for she wanted to find out if any members of her family had escaped Nasser or if they were still in Egypt. She had no idea that Michael had agreed to be part of the plan on the condition that Aron and Joshua would help find and bring his cousins to Israel.

Aron and Joshua had not reneged on their promise. They had used all their resources to find his family. The search started more than a month before, and they had found positive results. They didn't say anything to Michael, as they wanted him focused on what had to be done.

Hannah's brother and sister were alive with families. They were living in Alexandria. They had tried to leave Egypt, but financial and medical issues forced them to stay. They were actually expelled and had the necessary papers to leave Egypt. Reservations and finances suddenly appeared that would take them to Cyprus and then on to Israel. They would be arriving in the next few days. The promise had been kept.

Hannah totally broke down when she saw her family. It was her dream. Her prayers were finally answered. Doria was introduced to everyone and taken into the family with a warm reception.

Michael and Doria went through more debriefing, which took another week, giving Hannah and her family time to see Israel. Hannah's sister and brother decided to stay in Israel, for they were Middle Eastern people in mores and mentality. They had spoken Hebrew as children because of their father. It all fell into place.

Michael had one more thing he wanted to do. It would be more difficult. He needed help from the Company to find a way to bring Doria's mother to the United States.

Michael thought of the dad he never knew. "Where would I be if he had lived? How would my life be different?" He had, in a sense, done his part fighting for his people just as his dad had. He was able to strike a blow for good over evil, for decency over oppression, for freedom over tyranny. He was proud of what he had done and humbled by the fact that he was able, in some way, to make the difference.

He wanted to get back to his vision and dreams, to build a life with Doria. Michael felt he had fulfilled a promise to himself and, more important, to his dad and to Israel. He had done what he set out to do, in spite of the obstacles, the dangers, the pressures, and the personal consequences.

He finally knew who he was.

THE END

CPSIA information can be obtained
at www.ICGtesting.com
Printed in the USA
BVHW06s0352010618
517698BV00002B/2/P